GO LOVE'N HEART

Best Wishes

GOT A LOVE'N HEART

L. Martin

TATE PUBLISHING
AND ENTERPRISES, LLC

Got A Love'n Heart
Copyright © 2013 by L. Martin. All rights reserved.

No part of this publication may be reproduced, stored in a retrieval system or transmitted in any way by any means, electronic, mechanical, photocopy, recording or otherwise without the prior permission of the author except as provided by USA copyright law.

The opinions expressed by the author are not necessarily those of Tate Publishing, LLC.

Published by Tate Publishing & Enterprises, LLC
127 E. Trade Center Terrace | Mustang, Oklahoma 73064 USA
1.888.361.9473 | www.tatepublishing.com

Tate Publishing is committed to excellence in the publishing industry. The company reflects the philosophy established by the founders, based on Psalm 68:11,
"The Lord gave the word and great was the company of those who published it."

Book design copyright © 2013 by Tate Publishing, LLC. All rights reserved.
Cover design by Allen Jomoc
Interior design by Mary Jean Archival

Published in the United States of America

ISBN: 978-1-62295-461-2
1. Fiction / Coming of Age
2. Fiction / Romance / Contemporary
12.11.29

Acknowledgments

Cover photos by Chris' Photography
    Christie Robins, photographer
    115 W. Washington
    Osceola, Iowa 50213
chrisphotography.net

Thank you to Chris for taking the pictures, and to Brock and Cassi for posing and allowing their photos to be part of this project.

Also, I want to express a special thank you to my wife, Jodi, for her support and help with this book.

Introduction

As one travels the United States, the diverse beauty of the continent becomes apparent. You must allow yourself time to pause and appreciate that magnificence. All too often, we fail to take time to admire that which surrounds us; that to which we are accustomed or that which lies between where we are and where we want to be. I grew up midst the rolling hills of Southern Iowa and Northern Missouri. Although I did see the beauty embedded in the countryside, I never likened it to more romantic places depicted in books or shown in documentaries. As I have aged and seen a bit more of this land and the world in general, I have come to understand the meaning and import of the phrase "beauty is in the eyes of the beholder." I am not certain everyone can make that same comment with the strength of conviction that it deserves. Nonetheless, I take a measure of confidence in likening the beauty of Southern Iowa to the Pacific Northwest or the mountains of Colorado. True, a mountain in Colorado may conjure a different image than one in Southern Iowa—here a mountain is a very steep hill. The point being, it is all in the eyes of the beholder.

Southern Iowa is the place of my youth, the backdrop for my story. The story itself is fictional, although, in all fiction there lies a grain of fact. In my story, that grain of fact is derived from rural America, not the suburbs or inner city of a huge metropolitan area. The extent to which this matters is again in the eye of the beholder. Experiences will vary, but there is something shared when it comes to matters of the heart.

Chapter One

The summer had been a green one. The pastures were lush and crops were good. We hadn't had to contend with a drought for several years. Temperatures were tolerable; daytime highs in the mid eighties to low nineties. All in all, it had been a bearable summer. Now would come August and the dog days of summer. Iowa can be hot, but it's not the heat, it's the humidity that can make life uncomfortable. The Iowa corn tends to sweat, and that helps to raise humidity levels. The state fair had just ended and thoughts had turned toward volleyball and football, and oh yeah, that first day of school.

Back to school ads had bombarded consumers since the last week or so of July. Now the day had finally arrived. It is a curious phenomenon going back to school. Most kids can't wait for the last day of school, yet are ready—maybe even eager—to get back. Perhaps, filling every day of the summer months is not as easy as one might imagine. Whatever the reason, there is a certain excitement in the air that first day back.

Hillcrest High is no different than most other high schools. It is the only high school serving the communities of Torrence and Highland. The larger of the two is Highland, population 2,400 as of the last census. The school itself is located just outside of town on a hill that overlooks a valley. It is a picturesque setting, no doubt unappreciated by most of the student body. Even so, many art students have used the Hillcrest scenery as the topic of a project.

On this day, students began filing in with the usual chatter. The counselor and two other teachers were stationed in the commons handing out schedules while exchanging pleasantries, "How was your summer? Great to see you, I love your hair!" They also pointed students toward the auditorium for *the assembly*.

Common practice was to have an assembly to start the year. Here, the principal welcomes students back and reviews the handbook, any new rules, room changes, etc.

Seated in the fifth row was Chaz Thomas. Chaz was a senior, blessed with a little talent, and an abundance of confidence—maybe not as much talent as confidence. He could be—and often was—a jerk. He played quarterback for the football team and often had that know-it-all attitude. He never met a stranger. This, in and by itself would not have been such a bad thing. Problem was, Chaz never seemed to shut up. He loved to talk, mostly about himself. If he wasn't talking about himself, he was asking questions incessantly, trying to endear himself. Chaz wasn't all bad. He was the type of person who had to be accepted despite his shortcomings; and there were many who did. After all, he was his team's quarterback. His family was fairly well off, not necessarily wealthy, but they seemed to have plenty of money. Chaz drove a newer car and would always talk of trading for something better.

Seated to the left of Chaz was Denny Driver, a fellow senior. They had been friends for years. Some might call Chaz the dominant one. However, Denny would let Chaz know what he thought. Occasionally, Chaz would even listen. Denny was a likeable kid, always there for others, the total opposite of Chaz. Why they were friends is uncertain. Each seemed to fill some need for acceptance that the other had.

Denny was describing an issue he was having with his car, when Chaz interrupted. "Hey, look who just walked in! Hotties at ten o'clock."

He gestured to two girls just entering the auditorium, Teri Jane Hancock (Teej to those who knew her) and Katee Lynn Roberts (Teej would call her K, but she was the only one who did). They were also seniors. Both were attractive, intelligent young ladies, and the very best of friends.

The four had known each other for more than twelve years. They often referred to themselves as the "Gang." The "Gang" handle came about one summer following sixth grade when some older kids were bullying Chaz. The other three: Katee, Teej, and Denny came to his defense and the four united. "Don't mess with our gang," one of them said. The rest is history. It seemed to cement the beginning of a lasting friendship among the quartet.

When they were sophomores, Katee and Chaz dated for a while. Nothing serious, they went to a couple movies without the rest of the gang, so Chaz thought it counted. Now, Teej and Denny were getting especially close. They publicly denied it of course, but there were signs. Katee would nudge Teej to be more open. Teej wasn't sure that was what Denny would be comfortable with, and so it went.

Teej and Katee made their way to the row where the boys were sitting. Teej gave a little wave and subtle smile to the guys, mostly though to Denny. Denny replied with a nearly unseen wave of his own, the expression on his face betraying the fact that he really was glad to see Teej.

Chaz, on the other hand, was not so subtle. "What's shake'n ladies?"

Katee just shook her head, ignoring the greeting. "Hey guys, are we ready for this?"

"I'm always ready," said Chaz.

Teej slid into the chair next to Denny, whispering, "Hi," as she did so. Denny answered with a nod and a fidgety "Did you get your schedule?"

Before anything else could be said, Chaz intervened, "Move over, Bubba. I want to sit by Katee." Chaz stood up, expecting Denny and Teej to comply.

Denny was just a little annoyed. He was used to Chaz and Chaz's ways. This time, however, Chaz wasn't going to get his way. "Sit down. You can sit by her later," Denny said in an agitated tone. "This thing should be about ready to start."

"I just wanted to tell her something," Chaz said as he dropped back into his chair.

Katee nibbled the end of her finger, chuckling. *Poor Chaz*, she thought. It was at about that time she caught sight of a student she did not know. He found a spot more toward the front of the room.

"Who's that in the red tee?" asked Katee.

"He's a new kid," Chaz was quick to answer. "His name is Tyberius Henry, came from Indiana with his mom and sister. His dad was killed in a helicopter crash or something. So they moved here to be with his grandpa."

Denny felt obligated to chime in, "He goes by Ty, and he is out for football."

"Is he very good at football?" Katee asked, still looking toward the newcomer.

"He's pretty go—," Denny started, before being interrupted by Chaz.

"He's not all that great, average hands, so-so speed, and I don't think he likes to hit."

Denny countered, "If you throw them to him, he can catch them. And as for speed, he was third in the state meet in the four hundred, last spring."

"That was in Indiana."

Now Teej dove in, "Oh, and I suppose they can't run in Indiana."

Chaz bristled. "I bet I could outrun him in the hundred."

"Chaz, you are so full of it." Katee laughed.

"Well, you don't run four hundred yards down a football field," Chaz said. "Besides, he's a dork."

"Doesn't look dorky to me," Katee said, looking Ty's direction again.

"You wouldn't know. You're too stupid."

"I'm smarter than you think, Chaz. I know you're a dork."

Katee squirmed in her chair, trying to become more comfortable. Not that the seats were uncomfortable, she was just annoyed by Chaz. She looked to the stage. Nothing was happening yet. Her eyes moved around the room. There were still a few stragglers meandering into the auditorium.

Teej had just said something to Denny, while Chaz pouted before greeting a student who had just sat in the seat to his right. Finally, Katee's eyes rested on Ty—the new student. He seemed uneasy, gripping a notebook with pencil in hand. It was as though he was prepared to write down some important information that the principal was about to share. *I could tell him*, Katee thought, *he won't need to take any notes at this assembly, never have had to anyway*. She smiled at the thought.

Teej punched Katee's leg, whispering, "Don't stare."

"I am not staring," Katee said in a whisper of her own. As she did so, she turned to face Teej. Teej had her best who-do-you-think-you-are-kidding look on her face. Katee gave a toothless grin as if to say, "Okay, I'm busted. Don't be so smart."

The principal, Mr. Harris, was now at the podium. The students' commotion quickly subsided, replaced by an attentive silence. He started, "Good morning." About half the crowd gave a less than enthusiastic, "Good morning."

"That was weak," he said. "Let's try that again. It is only the first day after all."

This time the response had more life. "Much better," he said.

He spoke for about forty minutes, covering handbook items and changes, taking questions from students as they arose. Finally, he introduced new staff members and the eight high school students new to the district.

"Lastly, we have one new senior, Tyberius Henry." Ty stood up, as had the others before him. The student body clapped. Someone in the back of the room shouted, "All right, Ty! Go football!"

Katee glanced toward Ty, noticing how he blushed. He must have stood six feet, trim—the look of an athlete. No, she did not think he looked dorky.

Mr. Harris continued, "Ty comes to us from the state of Indiana. That is not at all bad. After all, it begins with an 'I' and ends with an 'A'." He had hoped to draw a laugh, but the students didn't seem to share his sense of humor. He cleared his throat and continued, "Now, let's make all of our new students and teachers feel welcome and have a fantastic year. We will start with the section on my right. You are dismissed to your first period class."

It was as close to orderly as it gets. School was underway.

They were off and running. The halls filled with students as they made their ways to first period classes. The hallway ruckus included the banging of lockers and laughter, along with a good helping of, "Hey, where are you going first period?" and such questions as "Are you taking American Lit?" Katee already knew that Teej would be in all of her classes, with both Denny and Chaz joining them in economics/government. She would discover that Ty would be in three classes with her and Teej, namely, physics, advanced math, and economics/government. They had just one teacher who was new to Hillcrest, a PE teacher.

In some of the classes, teachers did ice-breakers, little things to get students feeling they were back in school. For example, in advanced math class they reviewed parallelograms during the course of which, the teacher, Ms. Alnor, drew a square on the board, then asked, "Okay, suppose the length of one side is seven, I forget, what would that make the length of the diagonal?"

Katee fired her right hand into the air.

Ms. Alnor nodded to acknowledge her.

"Seven square root of two," answered Katee.

"Good job."

"Bam!" said Katee with satisfaction, snapping the fingers of both hands simultaneously.

Teej, who was sitting in the next row, held up her hand so Katee could give her a congratulatory slap, saying, "Oh yeah!

Big time!" After Katee had slapped her hand, she added, "That's my bff."

The class broke into a mild laughter. Katee noticed that Ty had been amused by the happenings as well.

"Hey, I don't get them right all the time. So when I do, it's cause for Cel-e-bra-tion time, come on," she sang the last part adding a little chair dance for effect.

Again there were giggles around the room. Katee looked toward Ty to gauge his reaction. She was pleased to see he was smiling back at her. She smugly turned her attention back to Ms. Alnor, who retook control of the class.

"And we do love to see the energy. Now, explain how you arrived at your solution."

Katee swallowed. "I hate this part."

Again, there were a few giggles, followed by Katee accurately explaining how she arrived at her answer.

"Very good. Now how else can we arrive at the solution?"

Someone else's turn, Katee thought, as she stole a glance Ty's direction, this time, a little disappointed to find him not looking back. Back on task, the remainder of class flew by. The bells rang, followed by the race to the lockers.

Before long, it was week four of the school year. The football team was two and one. The volleyball girls were still unbeaten. Not a bad start for fall sports.

One morning, Katee was at her locker. Ty walked by. Katee said hi. Ty may have mumbled something and went on to his locker.

Teej was a few steps behind Ty. She stopped beside Katee. "Did he say anything?" she asked.

"He said 'Hi' I think. Maybe. Or something." Katee shrugged. "I'm not sure."

"You know you seem to be…*interested*…in him," Teej said.

"No, I'm not," said Katee, as she dug a book out of her locker. Then she turned to be confronted by Teej's glare that seemed to be saying, "Who do you think you are kidding, girlfriend?" Katee felt compelled to add, "Well, maybe a little. I hate it when you give me that look."

"Psst, then don't try to yank my chain. Anyway, he hardly talks," Teej said.

"Some guys talk too much. Besides, what would be wrong with getting to know him? I bet we'll be put in a group and have to work together."

"Probably," said Teej, then changed the subject to the physics assignment.

Later that day, the girls were at lunch. Katee sat at a table with Teej and three other girls. The boys sat at a nearby table. That way they could talk football, cars, or whatever, yet still be close enough to converse with the girls if needed, and vice versa.

Regardless, Katee noticed, not for the first time, Ty was eating by himself. There were others in the area, but he wasn't talking to any of them. It was more like he needed a spot and found one in the middle of some other kids. Katee took a deep breath and said, "Teej, come with me."

Taken off guard, Teej was at a loss. "Ah…what?"

"Come on," said Katee, standing with her food tray in hand.

Teej took a quick swallow of milk. "Guess I'm following her. See you guys later."

Chaz took note of the girls' exit. "Where are those two going?"

"Maybe the bathroom. You want to join them?" was the response from a fellow football player.

Chaz snorted. "Think they'd let me?"

That drew some laughter from the table.

"Oh, I see where they're going. They're so stupid." Chaz watched as they found spots at the table where Ty was sitting with two sophomores.

"Hi," said Katee, taking the chair next to Ty. Teej followed suit next to Katee.

"Ah, hi," said Ty, pausing from taking a bite of salad. He was surprised by the arrival of the girls, as were the sophomores. The sophomores kept eating, though.

"Yeah, I was wondering if you got that math assignment done." Katee twirled spaghetti on her fork.

Ty replied, "Yeah, I did," still feeling caught off guard, not knowing exactly what to say. "Not sure how right it is, but I got it done."

He tried to be modest so as not to give the impression that he knew too much.

"We were wondering about number four," Katee said after finally taking a bite of the spaghetti.

Teej nodded in agreement. "Yeah, we got different answers." All the while she was thinking, *What was number four? I hope you've got this covered, K. From here on, I got nothing.*

"I don't really remember," was all Ty could think to say. "She'll probably go over them in class."

"Oh yeah, she usually does. We can find out then," Katee said. That would take care of the math problem discussion for now. Teej was relieved.

"I've been meaning to ask you, how do you like Hillcrest?"

"Ah, it's okay, takes a little adjusting. But it's fine."

"Where you came from, is it bigger than here, or smaller?" Katee asked.

"The school was about the same. Town was a little bigger, but we didn't have two towns sending kids to the same school," answered Ty. About that same time, the bell rang.

"Guess it's time to go, huh?" Katee said.

"I suppose so," Ty said.

"Well, see ya," Katee said, a little annoyed that their conversation was ending so abruptly.

"Sure thing," said Ty as he got up to take care of his tray.

After Ty had left, Teej leaned to Katee. "Guess it's a start."

"That's the way I see it."

Katee was proud of herself for taking the first step. She was not a shy person. However, her confidence level at times could use some bolstering.

Ty took a quick glance at the two girls as they took their trays. Why did they come to his table? Probably they were just trying to be nice. He didn't know if he could do that, approach someone he didn't really know and just start talking. Of course, they are in his class. Maybe they did wonder about the problem. He wished he could have been more helpful. Oh, well.

Football practice went well that evening; they finished early. Ty went straight home. Home was at his grandpa's farm. It was only a couple of miles from Highland. The farm wasn't very large, only 160 acres.

Grandpa was Tyberius Luke Henry, after whom Ty was named. (Ty's full name was Tyberius John Henry.) Around home he was called "GPa." He raised a few cattle and chickens, plus he had a couple of horses. Most of the ground was in hay or pasture. It wasn't a lot, but GPa was happy to have his son's family move in. GPa had lost his wife to natural causes two years earlier. At the time, he was asked about moving to Indiana. He declined, saying they would have to drag him off the farm or bury him there. He insisted it would be the latter.

Ty's father, John, was GPa's only child. John was in the Indiana National Guard. He was a passenger on a helicopter practicing maneuvers, a little over a year ago when an electrical failure caused it to crash. All six on board were killed.

Ty's mom, Mary, said she wouldn't blame anyone. John was serving his country and accidents happen. Even so, she would prefer that her children not enter the military.

GPa told Mary he could use some help on the farm. There was plenty of room in the house. He could use some help with the garden and chores. Mary believed there was room in the house, but not so much the part about needing a lot of help. GPa was pretty independent. On the other hand, she was concerned about her children, Ty and his older sister by one year, seven months, and fifteen days, Trace. They all took the sudden loss of their loved one very hard.

Mary did some research. She found there was a hospital in Highland where she could get a job as a nurse, and a nearby community college for Trace to attend. Of course, Ty could finish his senior year at Hillcrest. The three discussed it. They hated to leave friends and uproot what they had come to know, but for financial and emotional reasons it seemed best to move to Iowa. So they did.

Trace began commuting to the community college about twenty-five miles to the west of Highland. She also found a part-time job to help with money matters. In fact, even Ty had a part-time job at a grocery store in Highland. He worked weekends, although not every weekend.

It was Thursday evening. Ty had been home long enough to help GPa with some chores and get cleaned up. Mary was putting the finishing touches on the evening meal. Trace had set the table; Mom told her to go relax for a bit. She would call them in a few minutes.

Trace walked into the living room. "Hey little bro, what-cha reading?"

Ty looked up, turning the magazine that had held his attention so she could see.

"Ooooo, a tractor," said Trace. "Good thing there are pictures."

"Ha, ha, funny," Ty said. "You should be on TV. Well, maybe radio."

"Now that was funny," said Trace, taking her turn in the badgering. "So what do you know? We haven't talked for a while. How's school? Are you getting to know anyone?"

Ty was still looking at the magazine when he answered, "It's okay. And there is this one gir…" He stopped before finishing the sentence. Did he really want to share this with Trace at this time?

Trace's face lit up. A cougar ready to pounce. "Did you say… girl?"

"Nope," Ty said. "You must be hearing things."

Trace slid onto the couch next to her brother. "So, she got a name?"

"I suppose." Ty turned his back to his sister. "First, last, and middle, I would guess."

"Okay, guys, GPa's here. Time to eat," Mom called from the kitchen.

Saved by the dinner bell, Ty thought as he closed the magazine, leapt to his feet and headed toward the kitchen-dining area.

Trace chuckled to herself. "My little brother's got a crush. How can I find out who it's on?"

Ty put an arm around his mother. "All right, Sloppy Joes, my favorite!" Then he gave her a kiss on the cheek.

Trace chimed in as she followed Ty toward the table, "You don't have favorites. You even like horse meat."

Seated at the table, GPa joined the fray. "In that case, you stay away from my horses. And where's my kiss?"

Trace threw her arms around GPa's neck, giving him a big kiss on the cheek. "Love you, Grandpa."

Ty, acting incredulous, pretended to take offense, "Trace, he wanted me to give him the kiss."

GPa shook his head with a wrinkled face.

"But GPa, I'm hurt," Ty played along.

Trace stuck out her tongue at her brother. They all laughed.

Mom said a short prayer before they all dove into supper. This was a practice that was relatively new in the Henry home. It started after GMa had passed away. Now it was a custom.

The meal was nearly over when Trace spoke up, "Oh, I just remembered, Saturday afternoon I need to go over to Keri's to study for a while."

"Who is Keri?" Mom asked.

"Keri Roberts," Trace answered. "We are working on accounting. She has a sister at Hillcrest, in Ty's gr…" Trace slowed her speech as she noticed Ty had unexpectedly dropped his eyes toward his plate. Was Ty avoiding making eye contact with her? "ade. Ty maybe knows her. Katee, Katee Roberts?"

"Ah…yeah, she's in a couple of my classes," Ty said, then stuffed a bite of pie into his mouth.

Trace was watching her brother, now more closely than before. As Ty worked over the bite of pie, his eyes remained on his now mostly empty plate.

Oh, he knows Katee, Trace thought. "She's kinda cute, don't you think?"

Ty swallowed the pie. He took a drink of water and cleared his throat. "Yeah, I guess so." Then he excused himself as he moved from the table toward the living room.

A big grin spread across Trace's face.

Mom asked, "What are you smiling so big about?"

"Well, I am not sure. But I think I just figured out a secret," said Trace, proud of herself.

Chapter Two

Around two o'clock on Saturday afternoon, Trace arrived at the home of Keri Roberts. The two had known each other for only a couple of weeks, but had quickly become friends as well as classmates at Southern Community College. Both were enrolled in a two-year business program. They had started commuting together to and from school whenever their schedules allowed. They hoped to get their work schedules in sync so they could share the ride more often. Today they were studying for an accounting test. They had worked for an hour or so when it was time for a break.

"Time for some chips and salsa," Keri said. "What can I get you to drink?"

"Just water will be fine. I've been getting too much sugar at school," said Trace.

At that moment, Katee came in from outside. "Hi guys," she greeted the two girls. "Oooh, chips and salsa, don't mind if I do. Thanks." She helped herself to a sample.

"Hi and you're welcome," said Keri.

Trace also said, "Hi."

"Thought you were doing homework at Teej's place?" asked Keri.

"I was, but Denny showed up. You can tell who got the boot. Oh, well, best friends; ya got love 'em. I'll be upstairs, slaving away." Katee continued up the stairs to her room, calling back as she went, "Study hard."

"You too," said Trace.

She paused for a moment, then after some thought, continued, "What the hey. I might as well ask. I've got a question for you, that I might get in trouble for asking."

"Oooo, that's the best kind," Keri said, a little intrigued. "What's the question and why are you asking so hesitantly? I'm not sure that's a word—hesitantly, but you know what I mean."

"Yes, I do and I think it is a word," said Trace. "Is Katee seeing anyone, like as in a boyfriend, currently?"

"I don't think so. Why do want to know that?"

"You remember—I showed you a picture of my brother, Ty."

"Sure, oh my gosh! He likes Katee!"

"I think so," said Trace. The two shrieked with delight. "Problem is, he can be shy until you get to know him."

"Katee's not shy. Maybe we need to help them along," said Keri. "Katee! Katee Lynn, come down here a minute," shouted the older sibling.

Moments later, Katee appeared at the top of the stairway, "What are you yelling about?"

"Come down here. We need to talk to you." Keri motioned for her sister to join them. Katee complied, curious as to what this was all about. "Take a seat," said Keri, sounding more like an employer than a sister. Katee smiled, looked at Trace, then, dutifully sat down. She made a gesture, the meaning of which could only be, "Okay sis, what do you want?"

"Here's the deal," Keri said. "Do know who Ty Henry is?"

"Trace's brother? Sure," said Katee, shaking her head to the affirmative. "He's in a couple of my classes."

"What is your impression of Ty?" asked Keri while Trace tried to read Katee's body language.

"Ah…well." Katee's eyes wandered as she debated what to say. After all, this was her sister and the sister of the guy she had kinda thought about. "I haven't got to know him just yet. But we have talked a little. He seems nice."

"Let's cut to the chase." Keri leaned forward ready to get some answers. Katee's eyes widened as she feared the cross examination was about to rise to a new level.

Trace, on the other hand, burst out laughing. "You watch too much TV. Too much drama," she said. "Look, I think Ty likes you. He is awfully shy. Until you get to know him, that is. Then, he is nice, and can even be fun. I say that, even though he is my brother. I was just wondering if maybe you liked him back, a little. If so, maybe we could figure a way to get you two together. You know, for a date or something; since I know he is probably too shy to ask."

"Oh my gosh," Katee said. Her face reddened. *Oh my gosh*, she thought again, not knowing exactly what to say. *Do I come right out and 'fess up or do I try to be coy? Maybe I should tell them it is none of their business and to butt out.* Finally, she decided what to say.

"I'd go out with Ty sometime. I am not sure what he would say if he knew we were having this conversation, though. However, like I said, we've been talking some, so it's a possibility."

"That's all we wanted to know," said Keri matter-of-factly. "Now, do you want our help?"

Katee stood up. She still had a slightly embarrassed "this is great news" expression on her face. She thought for a moment, took a deep breath, then said, "No thanks, I think we're good. I'll give it a while, then see how it goes."

"Okay," said Keri, sounding a little disappointed. "But know we are here for you if you need any help."

"That is good to know," said Katee as she started back up the stairs. Abruptly, she stopped, turning back to the girls, "Oh, by the way, that was a nice rendition of good cop-bad cop."

"Gee, thanks," said Keri. "Who was the bad cop?"

"Ha, that's funny." Katee giggled as she made her way up the stairs.

Keri and Trace laughed as well.

Katee just made it into her room when she grabbed her cell phone. She had to tell Teej. This was big news!

The next couple of days, Katee looked for opportunities to talk to Ty. No such luck; she half expected Ty to say something to her. Surely, the older sisters had cornered him as well, giving him the third degree. Monday and Tuesday came and went with not so much as a "How's it going?" She was beginning to think she should have accepted Keri's offer to help, nah, maybe not—at least not yet.

Now it was Wednesday. Today was the economics field trip to the city. About a two-hour bus ride to some financial center. They would get the grand tour; a speaker would share how things worked in the business world. There were thirty or so taking the trip, plus the instructor, Mr. Charles, and the bus driver. Shortly after eight a.m., the students piled onto the bus, two to a seat. Katee and Teej sat together toward the back of the bus. Chaz and Denny were in the seat in front of them. Ty was a couple seats further up on the other side of the aisle. Todd Carson sat with him. Todd was on the football team, although he and Ty were not friends by any stretch. They would speak, but neither had a lot to say.

Ty spent most of the trip looking out the window. He could hear Chaz from behind. He was hard to ignore. A couple times Ty glanced over his shoulder. There was Chaz turned in his seat pestering, or flirting with Teej and Katee. Chaz reminded Katee how they had once dated, then, smirked about it. Ty looked back out the window thinking, *Why doesn't one of them slap him? Or is that just the kind of guy they like? I think I'm going to be ill.*

Chaz certainly gave ample reason to be slapped, but that never happened. What did happen was that Katee glanced in Ty's direction several times, hoping to catch him looking back at her. How does that song go? "I was looking back to see if she was looking back to see if I was looking back to see if she was looking back at me." Something like that. When they arrived at the financial center, Mr. Charles split the class into three groups, and no, Katee and Ty did not land in the same group. In fact, they hardly saw each other most of the day. Funny thing, not "ha ha" funny, but "odd" funny, they had looked for one another over lunch break, but neither saw the other or for that matter realized the other was on the watch for the other. At one o'clock the whole class was gathered in a large room—a small auditorium. A lady from the finance company spoke for about a half an hour, then answered questions for another thirty minutes.

During the talk, Ty spotted Katee four rows in front of him. Teej and Denny were there also, but no sign of Chaz. *That's odd*, thought Ty. Not to worry, Chaz was not lost. During the question and answer part of the presentation, Chaz had a question; he asked the lady presenting what her phone number was. A few chuckled, but not Ty. The lady said, "My husband doesn't like me to give that out." With no more questions, it was time for the long bus ride home. Mr. Charles reminded everyone to hit the restroom first, the bus was waiting out front, and they would leave in fifteen minutes.

Where he would sit on the bus was the farthest thing from Ty's mind. The class was scattered, not everyone crowding to get on the bus at the same time. It wasn't like there was a huge rush or anything. In fact, as Ty stepped onto the steps of the bus, there was not anyone immediately in front of him. Slowly, he moved down the aisle, scouring the partly-loaded bus. That was when he saw a particular empty spot. One person occupied the seat already, leaving room for one more. Teej and Denny were in the seat immediately behind the seat in which Katee sat alone! Ty was standing only a couple of seats from Katee when he froze in his tracks. *She's not sitting with anyone*, he thought. Just then, Katee raised her eyes, meeting Ty's. *Don't just stand there, dummy*, he thought. Ty took a breath, swallowed hard and asked, "Would it be okay if I sat here?"

"Sure," said Katee as nonchalantly as possible. She tried to remain composed, a toothless smile on her face. She glanced back at Teej, who mouthed the word *breathe* while fanning herself with her hand.

Ty had his back to Teej as he took his place in the seat next to Katee, so he was unaware of the communication between the friends. He rubbed his hands across his pant legs as he settled into the seat. His hands had suddenly become moist. Katee was now looking at him, trying to ignore Teej's antics, her best smile filling her face. *That smile*, thought Ty. *I don't have a chance*. Somehow, he managed a nervous "Hi," along with a weak smile of his own.

Katee returned an embarrassed, "Hi." Still smiling, a little uneasy, she thought, *Okay. What do we talk about? Do I let him go first? Maybe I should say something. It would help if I could stop smiling*. Katee was mid thought when Chaz came down the aisle.

The bus was mostly loaded by now, that meant the seats were mostly taken. Chaz immediately saw Ty sitting with Katee. "Hey, Ty, move up here so I can sit with Katee," said Chaz as if he was entitled to do so.

Katee looked to see how Ty would react. *Stand your ground*, she thought. *I want to sit with you.*

"Nah, I think I'm fine here," answered Ty. "We may have a lot to talk about. Then, who knows; we may decide that we like each other, after that, maybe a date. Who knows? Maybe a moonlit walk and some star gazing." Ty looked to see how Katee was reacting to his ramblings.

"All very possible," said Katee.

"Then, maybe we'll hold hands," continued Ty.

"Who knows?" said Katee, anticipating Ty's next words.

"After that, well, you know. Things could get real serious."

"I know where you are going with this. It's all very possible," Katee said, trying to keep a straight face.

"Yep, homework together," Ty deadpanned.

Katee lost it. She laughed out loud and clapped her hands. Teej and Denny looked at each other and shook their heads. Chaz grunted and found one of the few seats remaining.

The ride back to Hillcrest still took more than two hours. For Chaz, it seemed like an eternity. He pouted for a while, then tried to engage those around him in conversation. He kept looking back at the seat where Katee and Ty were. Most of the time, he could barely see them. The two had slid down in the seat, knees positioned on the seat in front of them. For Ty and Katee, the time flew by. What was it that Ty said? Something about having a lot to talk about, then deciding they liked each other.

The bus pulled into Hillcrest, then began to unload. Ty waited for the students across the aisle to leave. Then he stepped across the aisle to allow Katee to go, then Teej and Denny. Ty would be the last one off the bus.

Katee waited in the parking lot for Ty to get off the bus, hoping for a last word before he went to football practice. They were watching game film tonight since most of the seniors had been on the field trip.

Chaz saw Katee and felt obliged to say, "So did the dork bore you to tears?"

Katee gave him a stern look with no response.

Just then Ty emerged from the bus. He saw Chaz standing near Katee. *Not surprised*, thought Ty. "See you tomorrow," Ty said as he walked past Katee.

Chaz blurted out, "Oh I'll see you inside. We're watching game film, remember."

And you are calling people dorks. You've got to be kidding, thought Katee as she gave Chaz another irritated look. "See ya," she said to Ty.

"Hey, I'll talk to you tomorrow," Chaz called to Katee as she walked away. Katee made no comment. "Well, be rude," Chaz shouted, feeling snubbed.

Katee found Teej waiting at Katee's car; it was Katee's turn to drive. Katee forgot all about Chaz. Now was the time to talk with her bff and share this feeling that was making her giddy.

They got in the car and Katee said, "Kullllllllllllll."

"Come again?" asked Teej.

"Goggggggrl," said Katee, thumping the steering wheel and bouncing a little as she did so. It was like she was trying to speak, wanting to speak, but unable to speak because she was too excited.

"Oh my gosh! You're gurgling," Teej laughed. "Now I've seen everything."

"That was the best bus ride I have ever been on," Katee finally said, after composing herself.

"So did he ask you to go to homecoming?"

"Oh, you would have known if he had. I would have jumped over the seat and told you." Katee paused for a moment as she started the car, "I'm giving him 'til Saturday. If he hasn't asked by then, I'm asking him, and he'd better say yes."

Teej laughed. "And that's the way it's going to be."

"Darn right," Katee stubbornly said, shaking her head with an emphatic yes. "I like him."

That evening Katee told Mom, Deanne Roberts, all about the trip. She was a little reluctant to tell Dad, Thad Roberts, but she couldn't help herself sharing parts of her conversation with Ty. Her father picked up pretty quickly any unspoken suggestions there may have been. As Katee bounded up the stairs to her room, he winked at his wife and said, "I think she likes this b-o-y," spelling the letters.

Mrs. Roberts nodded in agreement. "I think you are r-i-g-h-t. Do you think we should talk to her about slowing down? She seems pretty excited."

"Ah, it was just a bus ride, and they were just talking. Too early to worry, let's find out a little about the boy first," Mr. Roberts said. "At least it's not Chaz Thomas."

"Good point."

Keri got home a skosh after nine. Katee heard her arrival and met her at the door. "Got some news," Katee said.

The next half hour, Keri was a captive audience. She didn't mind though. She saw something in her sister's eyes that somehow gave her a warm feeling. "Now don't go crazy. You've got a lot to learn about this guy," Keri warned, realizing that for as good as things seemed right now, it could hurt just as bad if things didn't work out.

"I know. I know," Katee said quickly. "It's just that while we were talking, it felt different. I felt confident. I don't know, like I didn't want that bus ride to ever end."

"Now that is crazy," said Keri. "I'm glad for you though. Just don't be unrealistic. Tomorrow will be a new day. Now we both need to get to bed. I need some sleep."

At the Henry house, there was a similar state of affairs. Trace entered the house about a quarter after nine, having dropped off Keri earlier. GPa had already gone to bed. Mrs. Henry, Mary, was at the dining room table mending a pair of GPa's coveralls.

Ty met his sister in the entry way. He greeted her with a huge hug and kiss on the cheek followed by, "How's the most beautiful sister in the world?"

Startled, Trace looked to her mom for explanation.

Mrs. Henry shrugged, "He's been like this all night."

"What have you done with my brother?" asked Trace.

Sounding incredulous, Ty said, "Can't a guy be nice to his sister and mother?"

"Don't forget GPa?" Mrs. Henry said, still working on her mending. "You gave him a hug, too. I don't think he let you kiss him though." She laughed.

"Good thing for that," said Trace. GPa thought Ty should not be giving him kisses. He was okay with Trace and Mrs. Henry giving him a kiss on the cheek as long as they didn't get too carried away. With an open hand, Trace looked squarely at her brother, and demanded, "Give it?"

"Huh," Ty said, trying to shrug her off. "I don't know what you are talking about."

"You know what." Trace had that "I'm your sister, don't you dare try to play innocent with me" look on her face.

Thing was, Ty really wanted to tell her. He was bursting at the seams to tell anyone who might care to listen and could try to understand. Unconsciously, he was wringing his hands, looking at his fingers for no reason other than he couldn't bring himself to look at Trace, or his mother.

Unable to stall any longer, he took a deep breath. "I talked to Katee." He glanced at Trace to see her reaction. She started to smile. "I mean, we really got to talk for a long time."

"And?" asked Trace. "How was it?"

Ty blushed. "It was good. It was really good."

Now, Trace was really smiling. Mom, also, was intent on listening in. Both were eager for more details. Ty gave them some satisfaction. He shared some of the things they had talked about, some of the things he had learned about Katee.

Katee and Ty went to sleep that night with thoughts of each of other, fully intending that they would see each other the next day without a wall between them. They would be like best friends, picking up where they left off the day before. That did not happen.

Morning came, and both were feeling great. They went off to school. When Ty entered the commons, Katee was there, surrounded by the Gang: Teej, Denny, and Chaz.

Ty couldn't tell what they were talking about, but he wanted no part of the conversation. He heard, "You're so stupid," from Chaz.

To which, Denny replied, "Yeah, and what does that make you?" *Well*, Ty thought, *maybe later*, but later never seemed to come. Katee seemed always to be occupied by others or something got in the way.

They almost got to at least exchange pleasantries one time. They were in economics when there was a brief lull at the end of class. Most of the class was just visiting. Katee went to sharpen a pencil. Ty's desk happened to be near the sharpener. Katee said, "Hey."

Ty nodded, straightening in his chair, then managed to say, "Hi, how's your day?"

"Pretty good." Katee smiled. "Say, do you know what's for lunch?"

Before Ty could say a word, Chaz, who was in the general vicinity, blurted out, "Pizza. If you don't want yours, I'll take it."

Ty didn't have a chance to get a word in. The opportunity to talk to Katee was lost.

Teej caught Katee at her locker just before her last morning class. "So have you talked to Ty yet?"

"No," said Katee, slightly agitated. "Maybe I'll get to at lunch." That didn't work out either.

Ty had a question for one of his teachers, then stopped in the library to look at a newspaper. At least, that was his reason for skipping lunch all together. Actually, it might have been that he was afraid Katee would be surrounded again and he wouldn't be able to say anything to her. This wasn't turning out to be such a great day for Ty. He didn't know how Katee felt, but he was beginning to think yesterday was as good as it was going to get.

Katee, on the other hand, scanned the cafeteria looking for Ty. No luck; he wasn't to be found. She shrugged to Teej, who looked around, then shrugged back at Katee.

Ty got home from practice and was just finishing some chores when Keri and Trace pulled into the driveway. This was Keri's turn to drive.

"Oh, so that's my sister's new heartthrob," Keri said, seeing Ty emerge from the barn. "He is cute."

Trace laughed. "You want to meet him?"

"Sure. I should check him out. You know…for sis."

"Uh huh…hey, guy," called Trace as they got out of the car. "I've got someone who wants to meet you."

"Oh, yeah," said Ty, walking toward the girls.

"This is Keri, Katee's sister."

They said hello to each other. "Wow, I should have known that. You and Katee do look like sisters." Ty felt the need to quickly add, "That's a compliment."

"Thank you. I will take it as such." Keri could detect that shyness in Ty. It helped that Trace was here, serving as a buffer. "I understand the two of you are getting better acquainted."

"I don't know," Ty said. "It's hard to get to talk to her. She's pretty popular."

Puzzled, Trace asked, "You didn't talk to her today?" Trace and Keri had already compared notes from last night's discussions with their respective siblings. They both anticipated hearing more regarding this blossoming relationship.

"Nah…there really wasn't any time." He couldn't help but sound a little dejected.

"Some of her friends aren't really very good friends. She's not as popular as you might think," Keri said, trying to encourage Ty. "She can make time for you. Just push some of those others out of the way."

Ty laughed. "I'll try to keep that in mind. Thanks. I can use all of the support I can get. It was nice meeting you."

"Same here," said Keri. Ty turned to go toward the house. He was out of earshot when Keri said, "If Katee decides she doesn't want him, I'll take him," winking at Trace.

"Uh huh," said Trace. "I bet you would. And you know what? I wouldn't blame you, but if you tell anyone I said that, I'll have to kill you."

"My lips are sealed." Keri laughed along with Trace.

Friday came and went. The boys won the football game, improving to five wins and one loss. Thoughts were turning toward playoff talk, although the coaches reminded everyone, "Three games still remain." For Katee and Ty, Friday was a repeat of Thursday.

It was now Saturday morning. Katee bounced down the stairs, finding Keri in the breakfast nook with a bowl of cereal, juice, and the daily newspaper in front of her.

"Where's Mom and Dad?" asked Katee.

"Remember, they were going to the city today, the races."

"Oh yeah, I forgot," said Katee pouring some juice and dropping a slice of bread into the toaster.

"I got to meet someone the other night," Keri said.

"Who was that?" asked Katee, buttering her toast.

"Trace introduced me to him."

"Ty?" Katee's interest was aroused. "You got to meet Ty?"

"Mmmhuh," answered Keri as she chewed a bite of cereal.

"What did he say? Did he say anything about me?"

"He said you are hard to get to talk to. There are other people hanging around you all the time."

"Just friends," said Katee.

"Yeah, right." Keri had her own opinion on some of Katee's friends. "Even I can tell, Ty is not comfortable in a group. You put four people together, and he'll feel smothered. You need to give him some room. Be more accessible. That is, if you want things to go further."

"Okay. I see what you are saying. I wonder if he is home today or working."

"Let's find out," Keri said, retrieving her cell phone from her purse which was nearby. She punched a couple buttons; it rang, and was answered by Trace. Then using her most mysterious voice Keri said, "This is the black widow. Is the target in sight?"

"What?" asked a bit confused Trace.

"Is Ty there?" said Keri in plain terms.

"Oh, sure. He's doing chores."

"Roger that. The scorpion is on her way," said Keri back in character.

"You are such a geek," Katee said, shaking her head as she grabbed her bag and headed for the door. "I'm going to the Henrys."

"She just went out the door," Keri told Trace over the phone. "I thought I did good, but she called me a geek."

"The black widow, scorpion thing, yeah, that was a little weird, or geeky." Trace laughed.

They were still on the phone when Katee turned into the Henrys' driveway. She had never actually been to the Henrys' house. However, she knew where Ty lived. Trace was standing on the front porch, still talking to Keri. Katee got out of her car. Trace pointed toward the animal pen near the barn. Katee guessed that is where she would find Ty.

Katee wasn't as nervous as she might have been had they not spoken on the bus ride home from the field trip. Still, there was some apprehension, especially since the last two days didn't go quite the way she had hoped. As she neared the pen, she could hear Ty's voice.

"You are going to have to stop being so ornery. I said stop that. Ouch, you may never get your bottle." It sounded like Ty was having some issues, but he didn't sound angry.

Katee climbed on the wooden fence that encompassed the pen. "Having problems?" she asked with a laugh.

"Uh, oh, hi," Ty said. He made the mistake of turning his back on the calf, a two-month old crossbred, who lowered her head and butted him. Ty lunged forward, then turned to confront the calf. "You're not a nice animal."

Katee laughed.

Ty shot her a glance with a "don't encourage her" look on his face!

Katee slapped both hands over her mouth. "I'm not laughing."

Ty shook his head, "This is hopeless." He looked again toward Katee then reached into a bucket that was hanging on the fence. "So what are you up to?"

"Not much," was the reply. "Thought I'd see what you were up to. We haven't talked much since Wednesday."

"No, I guess we haven't." Ty pulled a calf bottle from the bucket. "Well, I'm glad you came. Do you want to help feed this little monster?"

"I'd love to," said Katee. "What do I have to do?"

"Come here and I'll show you, careful not to step in anything." Katee joined Ty. "Now hold this so she can't pull the nipple off, then hang on tight. She'll do the rest. She gets a little rammy."

"I noticed. Oh my gosh. I've never done this before." The calf began devouring its breakfast while Katee held on as she had been instructed. Ty kept a hand on the bottle as well, just in case. "You're a good calf. What's her name?"

"I named her Hard Times. GPa found her mom in the pasture trying to give birth. She was having problems, so we had to help her. We saved the calf but lost her mom."

"That's so sad," Katee said.

"Yeah, nature and nature's way I guess. Anyway, I call her Hard Times because she had such a hard time coming into this world. GPa says we may keep her to be a herd cow. Her mom and dad were both good animals." Ty patted Hard Times then added, "That is if I don't get too mad at her first and send her to the locker."

"Uh, you wouldn't do that." Hard Times had finished her bottle. Katee petted her, scratching her ears. "You're such a good calf, aren't you, Hard Times."

"Okay, now when I count three run for the fence," Ty said. "Ready… two… three." Ty and Katee bolted toward the fence.

Hard Times was in hot pursuit. The two scaled the fence—laughing as they did so—just moments before Hard Times pulled up behind them.

Hard Times bawled as if to say, "cowards."

Katee reached through the fence, petting the calf. "You almost got us. You're really fast." She turned to Ty, "That was so much fun."

Ty laughed. "Might not have been so much fun if she caught us, but this time we're good."

"Oh, the horses!" exclaimed Katee looking toward a small pasture on the other side of the barn. One horse was white, the other red.

"You're in luck. I've got an apple." Ty walked around the pen to where the bucket was still hanging on the fence. Retrieving the bucket, he rejoined Katee. He took the apple from the bucket, then with a pocket knife removed the core and cut it into half. Next, he sliced each half into smaller pieces, giving Katee half and keeping half for himself. Then they went to the pasture fence.

"The white one is Chastity, and the red one is Thunder, right?" Katee asked.

"You remember." Ty thought, *That means you were listening the other day.* "To be safe, we will stay on this side of the fence. They don't know you, and they are big animals. But we can feed them from here."

Katee was not going to argue with the man in charge.

Ty called the horses by name, whistling for them to come. They galloped toward the gate on cue. Ty fed his apple to Thunder, talking to her all the while and stroking her nose.

Katee followed suit, feeding her apple to Chastity while petting her nose. She also petted Thunder's nose, telling both how nice they were, and she really was glad they let her pet them. This was a big deal for Katee. Although she lived in a rural area, she was a town kid. She had a dog named Buster; but the closest she came to farm animals was to see them from the highway.

At last Ty said, "We should wash our hands unless you want to smell like calf and horse."

"Oooo, washing hands would be a good idea," said Katee. "Does it matter what kind of apples you feed the horses. I mean, do they like some better than others?"

"Gosh, I really don't know. They usually just get what I have to give them. Maybe I should experiment and see if they like some better than others."

"I could help you."

"Good, cause I have trouble with that scientific method." Ty laughed. "We can wash here at this hydrant." They both ran water over their hands. Katee playfully flicked hers at Ty, getting him just a little wet. "Hey, now you're acting like Hard Times."

"I'll take that as a compliment. Hard Times and I are friends." *Okay*, thought Katee. *Now is as good a time as any.* "Say, I was thinking. Actually, wondering. You know, homecoming is this week. Next Saturday night, there's the dinner and dance, and skits. It's pretty fun. Anyway, I was wondering if you were going, like, with anyone in particular and if not, would you maybe want to go with me?"

"Ah, sure, I knew it was this week. I thought you'd probably go with Chaz and the Gang or somebody."

"Oh, no," Katee said quickly. "They'll be there. Teej is going with Denny. I don't know who Chaz is taking, but it's not me." Katee felt a little panicked, fearing that Ty was about to say no.

"Well, yeah, I'd like to go."

"With me?" Katee asked, just to be sure.

"Yeah, with you, sure." Ty said, smiling. "What will I need to wear?"

"It is semi-formal. Do you have a sports jacket?"

"Yeah, I do."

"Great, that with slacks and you don't need a tie," Katee said. "I have to wear a dress. I've got a black one. I hope you like it." *Why did I tell him that?* Katee thought.

"I'm sure I will. There is a cost for the dinner, isn't there?"

"Yeah, it will be thirty dollars for the two of us, fifteen each. And since I asked you, I'll pay it. That's the way that works."

"Oh, really. Say, Katee. Would you go to homecoming with me?"

She giggled and said, "Yes."

"Great, then I'll pay the thirty dollars."

"Uh, okay," she said. "But you don't have to."

"I've got it. It's no problem. I'll ask mom about using the car. If not, Trace will let me use hers, unless you want to go in my old pickup."

"Well, we could take the pickup, but ask about the car," Katee said with a wink. "Or, we can take my car if we need to. I'm just saying."

"No to the pickup, huh?"

"No to the pickup, unless all else fails." Katee laughed.

Ty would need to be getting to his job. He was working this afternoon and Sunday afternoon as well. Katee would need to return home after a quick stop at Teej's. There was news to be shared. She might call Keri from Teej's as well.

Chapter Three

Another Monday:
Ty couldn't help but recall how last week had ended, walking into the commons only to find Katee with her friends, unavailable for him to talk to. He parked the truck, then thought, *I guess I'll just have to go in and see. What will be, will be.* He noticed Katee's car as he walked across the lot. *She's already here*, he thought, *probably had play practice.* Katee was a thespian. She enjoyed being in the school play. It was one of the things she and Ty had talked about on the bus ride. She suggested that Ty try out for the spring play. He was a little reluctant, that would be something he would have to think about. As he walked into the commons, his eyes turned toward the tables where Katee could usually be found, with the Gang. Sure enough, there they were. Naturally, Chaz was monopolizing the conversation.

This time, however, Katee saw Ty. "Gotta go," she excused herself with a look to Teej and an ever so slight nod of her head.

"Where you going?" asked Chaz. Receiving no reply from Katee, he asked Teej, "Where's she going?"

"She's going to talk to Ty." Feeling obliged to explain why, Teej added, "They're going to homecoming together."

"What?" said Chaz, sounding incredulous. "She's going with that geek? I was going to ask her."

"Looks like you're too late, Buddy," said Denny. "The early bird has gotten the worm, as the saying goes," adding salt to the wound.

Chaz just grunted as he watched Katee catch up to Ty.

Katee caught Ty before he reached the hallway. "Hi."

"Hi. You must've had play practice this morning."

"Yeah, we did," said Katee, pleased that Ty remembered she was in the play.

"How's that going?" Ty asked.

"Pretty good, we still have a few weeks to iron out some things, but we'll be ready come show time. You'll have to come watch."

"Yeah, I'll put it on my calendar. Right now, I'm looking forward to homecoming, first a ball game, then a dinner and dance." Then he added, embarrassing himself, "with you."

Katee smiled, glowing a tad. "Me too."

"I brought the money," Ty said. "Who do I turn it in to?"

"Mrs. Clark. I'll go with you." The two made their way down the hallway to Mrs. Clark's office. Mrs. Clark was the student council sponsor as well as a teacher. Katee knocked on the mostly open door.

"Come in, guys," Mrs. Clark said. "How are you today?"

"We're good," said Katee, taking the lead. "We came to sign up for the dinner and dance."

"Fantabulous. For the two of you, that will be thirty dollars, and you need to sign right here."

While Katee signed their names, Ty dug out his wallet, then the money. Handing the cash to Mrs. Clark, Ty said, "Here you go."

"Thank you very much. Now, do you know how to get to Mister Q's? That is where the dinner, dance, and everything will be held."

"I do," said Katee. "I'll navigate. Ty will drive. We'll be good."

"All right!" said Mrs. Clark. "You are all set."

"Thank you," Ty and Katee said in unison. The warning bell to go to class just sounded so they left Mrs. Clark to go to their lockers. The Gang was coming up the hall. Katee flashed a thumbs-up. Ty noticed it. He supposed the gesture was intended for Teej, but he had no way of knowing. He didn't give the matter a second thought.

He left Katee at her locker. "I'll see you later."

"See ya." Katee was pleased with how the morning was progressing. This was going to be a good day.

In fact, the entire week went well, complete with traditional homecoming activities. Katee and Ty managed to find some time daily to talk, at least briefly. Both were looking forward to Saturday. Ty had to keep reminding himself he had a football game to play first. It was no secret though, at either the Roberts or Henry households, the excitement was going to be Saturday evening.

Thursday afternoon after the school day had ended Katee and Ty walked to the parking lot and stopped by Katee's car.

"Mom said I can borrow her cell phone Saturday. I think she wants me to take it so she can check up on us," said Ty.

"That's okay. But how will she call if you have her phone?"

"Trace is going to leave her phone at the house Saturday evening. Said she is going to a movie with Keri. So there will be a phone at home."

"I see. You guys don't have a regular phone, do you?"

"No, just Mom and Trace have cell phones. GPa really needs to have one too."

"And you could use one as well," said Katee. "I never go anywhere without mine. Here, let me give you my number." She wrote the phone number on a slip of paper that Ty then put in his wallet. "Now you have a reason to get a phone. So you can call me."

"I wouldn't need an expensive phone," Ty started to explain when suddenly he heard a voice call to them. He recognized it right away.

"Hey, Katee, Ty." It was Chaz. "Guess what? I'm getting a limo for Saturday night. Dad's springing for it."

Katee seemed to perk up at the news, "A limo. Cool. What color is it?"

"Jet black, of course; it's got real comfy seats, a super sound system, and a fridge."

Ty politely listened as Chaz bragged about the limo. He tried not to be facetious, but he couldn't help but think, *Wonder if it has a toilet in it? Some buses do.*

It was what Chaz said next that got Ty's attention.

"There's plenty of room. We can all go together. Heck we could get three or four more in there if we want."

Katee saw Ty's body language change at the suggestion they all go together. Still, she asked Ty, "It's a limo. What do you think?"

Uneasy, Ty looked at Katee, hoping for some understanding and not disappointment, "I've already got it set up to take Mom's car."

"Your Mom's car!" Chaz said in disbelief. How dare he compare going to homecoming in your mom's car to going in a limo. "Just tell her you get to go in a limo. She won't care."

Stuck in a car with Chaz, even if it is a limo, *I'd rather be dead and riding in a hearse*, thought Ty.

"It's our first date." Not that that would mean anything to Chaz. Ty was hoping Chaz would just disappear and Katee would want to be with him more than ride in a limo.

Katee got the message. "Yeah, it is. We'll go in Ty's car. It will be good. Everyone will be at Mister Q's anyway."

"You've gotta be kidding," Chaz said indignantly.

"You can get some others to go in the limo," said Katee, not wanting to hurt Chaz's feelings. She knew how he could pout.

"Yeah, yeah. Your loss." Chaz stormed off. "I'll get some others."

Katee shook her head and shrugged.

"Look, I guess if you really want to ride in his limo…"

Katee interrupted before Ty could say more, "I want to go with you. So unless you plan to rent a limo we will be going in your mother's car, and that's just fine."

Ty felt better hearing Katee say that. He hoped she would not be disappointed to miss out on the limo. He needed to get to practice, so they parted company for the evening.

Friday came with a buzz in the air. Ty and Katee had not spoken as of yet that afternoon. In fact, he hadn't seen her other than in class.

Ty stopped in the library for a minute to check a word in a dictionary. He overheard a pair of voices. It was Teej and Katee. They couldn't see him because they were on the other side of a bookshelf.

"The limo will be great," Teej told Katee.

"Yeah, Chaz says the stereo is pretty spectacular."

Ty didn't stand around to hear more. Nor did he peek around the bookshelves to say hello. Instead, he made a hasty exit, a little bummed by what he had just heard. *I thought she wasn't interested in the limo*, he thought.

Had he waited, he would have heard Katee say, "You guys will have fun, but so will I. I wouldn't trade places."

"Yeah, but you're my bff," said Teej. "I want you with me."

"Let's see. Do I want to ride with bff or hot guy, hot guy or bff, bff or hot guy?" Katee teased, holding out one hand then the other. "I'm sorry, hot guy wins. I'm riding with Ty." Then she laughed.

Disappointed, although not surprised, Teej grunted. "Mmmph, guess I know my place."

Later in the day, Ty and Katee did have a chance to speak. They had been talking for several minutes when Ty decided he needed to bring it up.

"So, you still okay with taking my mom's car tomorrow night?"

"Yep," said Katee. "Is there some problem?" she asked, thinking it odd that he would have any doubt.

"Oh, no, I just thought if you felt like you were missing out, not going in Chaz's limo; well, what I mean is, I didn't want you to be upset with me for not going in the limo."

"Ah," Katee said, a little bewildered. "I'm okay going in your mom's car, as long as you are going with me. I'm even okay if we have to take your pickup, but I prefer going in a car. And, I said we could take my car if we needed to." Then more softly, "I want to go with you. How we get there doesn't matter. Besides, I don't want to go with Chaz and a crowd of others. Teej and Denny would be okay, but who knows who else he's inviting."

"Good. I just wanted to be sure. I'm looking forward to tomorrow night."

"Me too, pick me up about 5:30, maybe a few minutes before."

"Count on it."

"Great! I've gotta go. I have to work tonight, so I'm going to miss the game."

"That's the pits. Oh well, I can tell you all about it at the dance."

Katee playfully wrinkled her brow, "Yeah, sure. Like, I want to talk about football all night."

"Maybe not." Ty laughed.

"Maybe not," said Katee. "Anyway, good luck, and Go Hillcrest!"

The boys would win a hard fought game sixteen to fourteen. Ty scored a touchdown on offense when he made an acrobatic catch in the end zone. He also recovered a fumble while on defense that led to another Hillcrest touchdown. The team was successful on both two-point conversions.

On Saturday morning, Ty took his mom's car to the convenience store to fill it up with gas. Chaz drove in just as Ty was finishing. Ty thought, *Oh boy, look who's coming. My day is complete.* Chaz was becoming more and more of a thorn to Ty.

"Hey, Ty guy. How's it going?" said Chaz as he climbed out of his car.

"Just fine."

"Nice job last night."

He's trying to do a butter job. Wonder what he wants, thought Ty before saying, "Thanks."

If Chaz thought Ty was going to return the compliment, he was wrong. More than likely, Ty would have said something like, "If we only had a better quarterback, we might be able to put up a few more points."

"Is this the car you're taking tonight?"

"Yeah, it is," said Ty, trying to not be too annoyed as he replaced the gas cap.

"Sure ain't no limo."

"Nope, I guess it's not. When you're right, you're right." Just a hint of sarcasm creeped into Ty's tone.

"You know Katee really wants to go in the limo. Teej and Denny are riding with me. There'd be plenty of room for the two of you."

"Nah, I think we'll be okay. We talked about it. Shoot, she said we could even take my pickup if worse came to worst." Now, Ty was getting irritated.

"Okay, okay. Suit yourself. Can't say I didn't offer. So, did anyone give you directions on how to get to Mister Q's tonight?"

"Katee knows the way. We'll be fine."

"Ha. I wouldn't trust Katee to show me how to get to her house. Back when we were going out, I listened to her directions to get us to a mall for a movie. She got us lost. We missed the first twenty minutes of the show. Here, let me draw you a map." Chaz grabbed a paper towel from a dispenser and with a pen from his pocket, drew a map. "Take 61 north to the interstate, then east to Exit 21. Take that exit. Then go back north about 2 miles. Can't miss it, Mister Q's."

"Okay. Well, thanks. It's always good to have a backup, just in case." Ty folded the paper, and put it into his billfold. "Probably see you there tonight," he said, trying to be cordial as he got in his car. Next stop would be the car wash for a wash and vacuum.

Three thirty was showing on the clocks. Katee was getting anxious. She had decided earlier that three thirty would be when she would begin to get ready. She had been pacing since two o'clock. Now she could actually head for the shower.

"Finally," Keri told their mother. "She was starting to make me go nuts!"

"She is pretty excited," Mrs. Roberts said.

It was ten till five when Katee emerged for all to see. "What do you think?" she asked, hoping for good reviews.

Keri started to speak, but her mother clamped a hand over her mouth. "Never give your sister the opportunity to be critical. You look unbelievable. The boys will be standing in line to dance with you."

"Thank you, but there is only one boy I want to dance with."

"I wasn't going to be critical," said Keri, freeing herself from her mom with a smug look. "You look beautiful. Ty's going to think so too."

"I hope so," said Katee.

"Well, I need to go pick up your father. He was leaving his car at the dealer. They have to fix something," Mrs. Roberts informed the girls. "Be home by eleven-thirty."

"I know," said Katee, reassuring her mother with a kiss on the cheek. "Ty knows too, so don't worry."

"I'll be home by then too," said Keri.

Katee and her mother gave Keri a look, seeming to poke fun at the curfew that she no longer had.

"I want to find out how the date went." Keri laughed.

"I'll share all the details."

"You'd better. I've got to get going. I'm picking up Trace. We're going to a movie. It's a love story," she said, winking at Katee.

Katee returned an embarrassed smile.

Keri and Mrs. Roberts went out the door together, each leaving in a different vehicle. Katee took another look in the mirror, smiling at the teasing from her sister, and began rehearsing what she would say when Ty arrived.

Meanwhile, at the Henry house, Ty was doing some final primping of his own. He ran his comb through his hair then said, "That's as good as it's gonna get. What's the verdict?" He turned to face his mother and sister.

"Well," said Trace, with a lengthy pause. "If I weren't your sister, I think I'd go out with you."

"Now that is high praise," Ty's mother said, reaching over and adjusting the lapel of her son's sports jacket. "I couldn't agree more. You are very handsome. Don't forget the corsage. When do you have to pick her up?"

"A little before five thirty; I've got a few minutes."

"Yeah, you don't want to be too anxious. Just don't be late," Trace said.

"Not to worry. I'm leaving in just a few."

"Oops, there's Keri. I'm off." Trace started for the door, shaking a finger Ty's direction. "Remember, this is a first date. No smooch, smooch."

"Gotcha, sheriff." Ty chuckled. "You have to admit she is a little wacky."

"You don't mean that," his mother said, giving him a little swat on the rear.

Trace rushed out the door and climbed into the passenger side of Keri's car.

"So," Keri asked as Trace settled in. "How does he look?"

"Well, I don't want to brag. However, I am not so sure this Roberts girl is good enough for my bro. You know what I mean?"

"Oooooh. You just wait till he gets a look at my sis. Someone will have to help him close his mouth," Keri said.

"Oh, gross. What an embarrassing thing to say."

Both girls laughed.

Back at the Roberts house, Katee looked at the clock on the wall for the umpteenth time. It didn't seem to be broken, but it didn't seem to be moving along very fast either. She was back to pacing, glancing in the mirror each time she walked by. Suddenly, the doorbell rang. "Good, he's early." One last look in the mirror, and Katee went to the door.

"Chaz!" a bewildered Katee blurted out. "What are you doing here?"

Chapter Four

"Ty called me. Said he had to help his grandpa, and could I pick you up and take you to Mister Q's. Then he'll meet us there. So you ready to go?" Chaz had an impatient smirk on his face.

"I can't believe…" Irritated, Katee reached for her cell phone.

"You won't be able to call him. They were towing a tractor or something. He called from RJ's Repair. So you want a ride or not? Teej and Denny are in the limo."

"I don't have a number anyway. So he's going to meet us there?" Katee asked, still taken aback by this turn of events.

"Unless the dork can't follow directions, that's the plan."

"Okay, I'm ready." Clearly disappointed, Katee put her phone back in her bag and walked to the limo with Chaz.

"You really look good."

"Thanks." Somehow, the compliment didn't make Katee feel any better. She was debating with herself whether she should be angry with Ty or understanding that he needed to help his grandpa. Why tonight of all nights?

The limo driver held the door, saying, "Good evening."

Katee nodded, stepping into the car. Teej had moved to the empty seat so Katee could sit next to her, leaving Denny across from them to sit with Chaz. There were no other passengers in the limo. Guess Chaz couldn't find anyone else to share his ride, or maybe he didn't try to find anyone.

"Guess you heard about Ty," Katee said.

"Yeah," said Teej. "He's supposed to meet us there, so it'll be okay."

Katee's lips tightened, then she said thoughtfully, "He'd better'd be there. I don't see why a stupid tractor couldn't have waited till later."

An awkward silence followed. It didn't last very long. Chaz would have exploded. "Oh, I just remembered!" Chaz said. "Mrs. Clark said there are no cell phones allowed tonight."

"What?" Katee asked, awakened from her thoughts about Ty.

"Yeah. That's what she said. We can leave them here in the console. They'll be safe. She said they are going to take them away if they see anyone with one. Then you'll have to wait till Monday to get it back, so give 'em up. I'll put them in here. Just as well shut them off and save the battery."

Chaz placed his phone in the console. The others were a little reluctant to do so.

"Are you sure about this?" Denny asked. "I thought we got to have them last year."

"I don't know if we did or not. All I know is what the beast from the east said. So hand them over."

"This is ridiculous!" Katee protested. "They make it more like a prison all the time."

"Do you want to lose your phone?" Chaz extended his hand. "They'll be safe in here."

Reluctantly, the three turned off their phones and handed them to Chaz, who secured them all in the console.

"Now, we won't have to worry about losing them," Chaz said, reassuring everyone.

Chaz did his best, with some success, to lighten the mood. They arrived shortly before six. Upon entering, they were greeted by Tara James, a junior student council member who was checking off names.

"Katee, I thought you were coming with Ty."

"I was…I am. He had to help his grandpa, but he'll be here in a while. So we need a table for five."

"Not a problem," said a waitress. "Just follow me." She guided the Gang to a table, "When your fifth arrives, I'll bring him over."

"Thank you." Katee didn't want the others to think she was somehow taking charge, but she did not want Ty to be left out. "I'm not going to order until Ty gets here."

"We should at least get an appetizer. What do you think? Cheese balls or onion rings?" asked Chaz. "I'm hungry."

"They have fantastic cheese balls. That's my vote," offered Denny.

The girls agreed, so cheese balls it was.

The conversation picked up from what it had been in the limo, although Katee kept an ever vigilant eye on the entryway hoping Ty would appear. It was at about twenty after six, the cheese balls nearly gone, when Chaz got up and said, "I'll be back in a minute." There had still been no sign of Ty.

"Where is he?" Katee asked; the concern in her voice evident.

Teej tried to be reassuring. "He'll be here."

"Did you get to talk to him? I mean were you there when he called?"

"No," Teej said. "All we know is what Chaz told us. But he said he gave him directions. It's not like it is hard to find or anything."

"It's only six thirty. No reason to panic," Denny said. "I talked to him a little last night. He wanted to come. In fact, he was looking forward to it. He'll be here."

Katee felt a little better, but not much. She gave another glance at the entry then surveyed the room. She noticed a table to her left where a girl was texting. "Hey, I thought we couldn't have our cell phones?" Katee gestured toward the girl.

"Uh, that's a gyp," said Teej, seeing the girl with the phone. "We should turn her in to Mrs. Clark."

Denny was not quite so quick to send anyone to the gallows. "Or we could just warn her so she doesn't lose her phone. Be back in a flash." He got up and went over to the table where the offender was. It wasn't like she was alone. There were a couple of football players and other girls at the table as well.

"He is such a good guy," said Teej.

Katee just chuckled. "You really want to turn her in. Don't you?"

"Oh, yeah, you know I do."

"Me too." Katee giggled.

Denny wasn't gone long. "They seem to think it's okay to have their cells. So I don't know."

Just then, Chaz returned. "That lady at the desk; she said they got a phone call. It was from Ty. He's not going to be able to make it. Something about they were having problems and it was taking longer than they thought it would."

"What?" Katee asked. "He's not coming at all?"

"That's what she said. She stopped me, asked if I knew what group Ty Henry was supposed to be with. I said yes. She asked me to tell you guys he wasn't going to make it. And he said tell Katee to have a good time. That's all I know."

"This is just great!" Katee was miffed. "Guess we just as well go ahead and order and I am going to have a good time. It's not going to ruin my homecoming!"

So it was settled. Ty was not coming. The Gang would order their meals, enjoy and partake of the festivities. The matter of the cell phones was never brought up again that evening. However, Denny noticed other students with their phones. He thought it strange nothing was said to them. *Surely, Mrs. Clark had to see them. Was it possible Chaz had just been mistaken when he said they were not allowed?*

At about seven fifteen, after nearly everyone had finished eating, the activities commenced. The homecoming king and queen presided over the program. Each class performed a skit. Katee, along with three others, represented the senior class. All of the skits were well done. Voting was done by applause, so naturally the winner was the class with the largest numbers; that happened to be the seniors. The dance began immediately after the skits.

Everyone seemed to be having a good time. Mrs. Clark kept an ever watchful eye on the party goers, pleased at what she saw. She would visit with some of the students; that was her way. She had just filled her own glass with punch when Todd passed by.

"Hi, Mrs. Clark," Todd said.

"Well, hello, Todd. Are you having a good time?"

"Oh yeah, I think this is one of our better homecomings. It helped to win the football game."

"Certainly didn't hurt. You know, I don't see Ty Henry. I thought he was coming with Katee Roberts."

"I guess I thought so too. I don't know what the story is. She looks like she's having a good time, though. See ya around."

"Sure thing, Todd, enjoy the rest of the evening."

Todd rejoined the guys at the table from which he had come. The guys included two fellow football players, Jake Jones and Al Jordan. Al was the monster of the group. Two hundred sixty pounds, six foot four inches tall; he was large and in charge. In fact, he was being recruited by a couple of major universities. His grades were okay, although not great. He had to decide whether the support he might receive would be better at a larger school or a smaller one. Jake and Todd were not being recruited. They would have to work their way through college although they were having fun playing high school sports. They joked that some day they could say they knew Al way back when, after he made the big time.

As Todd rejoined the group, he asked, "Say, do you guys know what's up with Ty? Wasn't he supposed to be here with Katee?"

"I don't know," Jake scratched his chin. "But yeah, I thought he was coming with Katee."

"Yeah, he seemed to be looking forward to it," said Al. "They don't look like they're missing him any."

"They do seem to be having a good time, especially Chaz," Todd noted, gesturing toward the dance floor where Katee and Chaz were sharing a slow dance.

"Hey big guy, why don't you go cut in? You could rescue Katee, and ask about Ty," said Jake.

"I think I will." Al took a drink of punch and got up, without any further encouraging. He made his way across the dance floor to where Katee and Chaz were. It was like the parting of the sea, as the other couples made way for Al. Al tapped Chaz on the shoulder. "May I cut in?"

Chaz was a little annoyed, but Katee said, "Sure." After all, Al had been very gentlemanly. As she took his hand she added, "Just don't step on my toes."

"I'm a good dancer," said Al, pretending to be a bit offended. "Don't you know linemen are light on their feet?"

Chaz rejoined Teej and Denny. He grumbled as he sat down, "The big jerk."

Al asked Katee, "I thought you were coming here with Ty?"

"So did I. He had to help his grandpa. Guess I shouldn't be too mad at him."

"You've had a good time haven't you?"

"Oh yeah, I just wish Ty would have been here too."

Just then the music ended. Al thanked Katee for the dance. Katee thanked Al.

She glanced at her watch as she returned to the table, "It's ten till eleven. I need to be getting home. I'm sorry, guys."

"Don't be," said Teej. "We should be getting home too."

Chaz and Denny did not argue the point. The four went to the parking lot where the driver and limo awaited them.

Earlier, that same evening at 5:20 p.m.: Ty pulled into the drive of the Robertses' house. He took a quick look in the mirror to ensure no hair was out of place. He inhaled a deep breath, then with corsage in hand, got out of the car and walked to the front door. Katee's car was in front of the garage, so he knew he was at the right house. He rang the doorbell. A dog barked. *That must be Buster*, he thought. No one came to the door, so he rang the bell again. Still no answer, so he knocked on the door. He could see through some curtains. There didn't appear to be anyone home. Puzzled, Ty looked around aimlessly. This did not seem right.

Phone number, he thought. He found the number Katee had given him. Using his mother's cell phone, he dialed the number. The phone rang four times; then Katee's voice said, "This is Katee. Leave a message. I'll get back to you."

Ty left a message, saying he was confused and asking Katee to call him back to explain. He remembered Katee saying she always had her phone, so it should only be a matter of minutes before she called. That is, unless there was some problem. He started to imagine all sorts of possible explanations. Someone might be ill or hurt. What to do next? Should he just wait here?

A lady appeared in front of the house next door. "Well, hello there. Are you looking for one of the Roberts?"

"Yes, I was looking for Katee," Ty said politely.

"Oh, she left a little while ago with a young man. He had a fancy limousine. Mercy, I don't know where kids get the money for that kind of transportation."

Chaz! thought Ty before saying aloud, "I don't know either. Thank you."

Ty started for his mother's car thinking to himself as he went, *I don't get it. We talked about the limo, and she said it didn't matter.* As he got to the car, Ty remembered plan B. He got out the map that Chaz had made for him earlier in the day. He recalled having overheard someone talking about going north on 61 and Mister Q's being a couple of miles north of the interstate. Maybe Chaz's map would get him there or at least close. If Katee would just call, she could give him directions and explain what was going on. Ty put the corsage and his jacket in the back seat.

Even though Ty had not lived in the area for a long time, he knew where Highway 61 was and how to get to the interstate. However, he had never been to Mister Q's. He called Katee a second time, still no answer, so he left a message. He whispered, "Guess I'll see how good Chaz's map is." Ty had a nagging distrust of Chaz. There was something about him Ty didn't like. In fact, there were a lot of things that he didn't like about Chaz.

Ty drove north on Highway 61 to the interstate, then took the east exit. The first exit sign he saw was number 90. *Guess it'll be a little ways to twenty-one*, he thought. He didn't have a lead foot. To the contrary, he usually drove five or so miles per hour below the speed limit. His dad used to say, "It will still be there no matter how fast you go; and if it's not, it's just as well you weren't there when it went."

It was almost seven when he reached Exit 21. *Finally*, thought Ty as he blew out a huge breath of air. "I'm surely about there." As he drove north of the interstate, he looked intently, anticipating seeing a huge sign with a parking lot full of cars. What he saw first was a truck stop. It had a convenience store with places to get fuel and there was a McDonald's, but no Mister Q's. Well, Chaz did say it was a couple miles from the interstate. Ty was still concerned though. A sign said the town of Mitchell was three miles to the south, but no mention of Mister Q's. The countryside was pretty. A few houses dotted the landscape. It sure looked rural to Ty, just pastures and farmland. He had checked the odometer the moment he pulled off the interstate. He had gone about five miles when he decided that was far enough. Pulling into the next drive he came to, Ty called Katee's phone for a third time, then, turned around to go back the direction from which he had just come.

Ty decided he just as well get something to eat so he stopped at the McDonald's. There were several customers inside, but no line of people waiting to be served.

"May I help you?" asked a cute brunette from behind the counter.

"Uh, yes please. I'll have a number three meal." Ty then paid the girl. "Say, could you tell me how to get to Mister Q's?"

She thought for a moment, before saying, "I'm sorry. I've never heard of it. What do they have there?"

"It's supposed to be like a dinner club. There was supposed to be a dance there tonight."

"It's not anywhere near here. Pretty sure I would at least know about something like that."

His order arrived just then. He thanked the girl, took his tray, and looked for an open table. As he moved away, he heard some girls whispering. Couldn't really tell what they were saying, but he did make out the word "vavoom", whatever that meant. He pretended not to hear, but hoped if they were talking about him it was a good thing. As he ate his meal, his mind replayed the events of the evening. Just didn't make any sense, none at all.

The burger, fries, and drink were good. Not what he thought he might be eating this evening, though.

Don't feel sorry for yourself, whatever you do, he thought. *Maybe I should ask that girl for her phone number. Maybe she is about ready to get off work. Maybe that's a bad idea. Just as well head home.*

Ty removed the cell phone from his pocket, looked at it for a moment. It was as if he expected it to suddenly ring. Perhaps that was merely wishful thinking on his part. He dialed Katee's number. Same result as before. "This is Katee. Leave a message. I'll get back to you."

Ty left his fourth message of the evening, took care of his tray, and headed toward the exit. The cute brunette called to him as he neared the doorway, "Have a good evening."

"You too," he said. Nighttime had arrived in earnest, a full moon, with a sky full of stars to boot. Ty got into the car, and found a map in the glove box. Rather than take the interstate home, he found an alternate way, going south then back west. Had he taken the interstate, he might have noticed the sign for west-bound traffic directing travelers to Mister Q's.

It was shortly after ten when Ty pulled into the Henrys' driveway. He turned the motor off and stared at the moon for a full minute. He could see the face of the so-called "Man in the Moon." "I hope you're not laughing at me," Ty whispered. He made one final call to Katee, left a message, shut the phone off, got out of the car, retrieved the corsage, and walked to the house.

Ty's mom was in the living room reading. "You're home a bit early aren't you? I didn't expect to see you until a quarter to twelve."

"I know," was all Ty said. Opening the refrigerator door, he added, "You can have this." He held up the corsage for his mom to see before placing it in the refrigerator. Then he went straight to his room.

His mom followed him. "Ty…is something wrong?"

"I don't want to talk about it right now…please."

"Okay, maybe later; when you feel like it."

At about ten thirty, Keri and Trace pulled into the Henry driveway.

"Ty must be home," said Trace. "That's Mom's car."

"That's early for them to be back from Mister Q's," said Keri. "Wonder what the story is?"

"I don't know. But it is odd. I'll find out what's up. Talk to you tomorrow."

Trace got out of the car. Keri called to her, "I'll talk to Katee too."

As she drove off Keri thought, *Maybe Katee's there too. They may have stopped at Ty's for something.*

Trace saw her mother the moment she walked in the door. "Is Ty home?"

"Yes. And something has happened. He wouldn't tell me what. Go see." The look on her face filled in any words she left out. She knew how close her children were, and that there was a time for her to be involved and a time to let them find comfort in one another.

Trace knocked gently on Ty's door, peeking into the room as she did so, expecting to be invited in. Ty was sprawled on the bed—still fully clothed—staring at the ceiling. Clearly he was wide awake, but he didn't move a muscle as Trace slipped into the room. She carefully laid down on the bed next to him stealing a glance at him as she did so, hoping for some form of response.

After moments of silence that felt much longer, she finally said, "What's up?"

Ty took a deep breath but didn't say a word.

Disappointed in the response, yet undeterred, Trace asked more directly, "How was the date?"

"There was no date," was the exasperated reply.

"What do you mean, there was no date?"

"Just what I said; there was no date. She stood me up. She had already left with Chaz Thomas when I got there."

"You've got to be kidding!" Trace was incredulous. "There must be a mistake."

Ty shook his head. "There is no mistake." He then gave Trace an account of his evening. As he relived the evening, his voice would crack; he would fight back a tear, bite his lip to ease some growing anger and disappointment.

"I ought to go kick that little tramp's rear end," Trace said after hearing the story.

That caused Ty to smile briefly. "I don't guess that would change things any."

"Maybe not; but you deserve better than that." Trace turned on her side, putting an arm around her brother so she could gently hug him; perhaps easing some of the pain that he surely must be feeling. "I could get you a date with Keri," Trace offered.

"To be honest, I'm a little miffed with the Robertses right now, maybe at girls in general." Then he closed his eyes. "I'll keep the offer in mind, just in case I change my mind."

"You do that," Trace said, as she snuggled more closely to him.

Somewhere in the night, sleep finally overcame the two of them. Their mother checked on them, finding them both sound asleep; she turned out the light, content to know they were both safe. She would have to wait until tomorrow to learn the details of the evening.

At about 11:20 p.m., the limo was nearing Highland.

"Hey Teej, change places with me. Denny wants to talk to you," said Chaz.

"We can talk. We've been talking," said Teej with a little grimace on her face. She knew that Chaz just wanted to sit next to Katee. Teej didn't really like Chaz all that much, so if not letting him sit next to Katee annoyed him it was a good thing to do.

"So, what are you going to do about Ty?" Teej asked Katee.

"Oh, I suppose I will give him a second chance. But he'll have to make it up to me. What do you think? Flowers? Dinner?"

"Are you kidding? Chocolates. Definitely chocolates."

"You're right. Chocolates. Yep. Flowers too. And dinner." Katee laughed.

"You've got to be kidding. You are so stupid," said Chaz. "The dork stood you up, and you want to give him a second chance. Good grief."

"He was helping his grandpa. I'm not going to be mad at him for that. Besides, he missed out on a great evening."

The limo came to a stop in front of the Robertses' house.

Katee started to get out, then remembered, "My cell phone."

Chaz handed out all of the phones to their respective owners. "You had a good time, right?" Chaz asked as he followed Katee out of the car.

"Yes, I had a good time."

"Then shouldn't I get a little something?"

"You're right." Katee turned to face directly toward Chaz. "Thank you for the ride. I had a great evening. It was fun. Here is a little something for you." Then she winked at him. "See you guys." Turning, she left a bewildered-looking Chaz and half-ran up the drive, smiling to herself. She paused for a moment at the door to give a final wave before her friends drove off.

Chapter Five

Keri peeked through the curtain as the limo drove away. She couldn't hear what was being said, but none of this looked right. A little pang of anger came over her as she awaited Katee's entrance into the room. *She'd better have a good explanation for this*, Keri thought.

Katee had given a final wave to her friends before opening the door. The lights were on in the house. Katee expected her parents to be waiting up for her, one eye on the door, the other on the clock. She would not be disappointed. The two of them were at the kitchen table, each nursing a glass of warm milk.

Katee tapped her watch. "Eleven twenty-nine; a full minute to spare."

"More like twenty-four seconds," her father said, pretending to be grumpy.

Her mother fought back a smile. "Never mind him. How was your evening? Did you have fun?"

"Yeah, it was good," she said, sampling the milk from her father's glass. "Gag, that's awful. How do you guys drink this stuff?" She shivered, then added, "Everybody seemed to have a good time."

Her dad tapped his cheek with a fatherly glare. Obediently, Katee responded by giving each parent a kiss on the cheek.

Katee turned toward the living area where Keri was waiting, as she did so she turned on her cell phone.

"So how was Ty?" Keri asked impatiently.

"He didn't get to come," Katee said, half listening to Keri and half focusing on her phone. The telltale sound of messages being delivered to her phone got her attention. "Oh, my gosh. I've got five messages." She kicked off her shoes as she skillfully punched the buttons to listen to her voice mail.

"I don't understand. What do you mean he didn't get to come? When I picked up Trace he was dressed and all ready to go." Keri demanded answers, but her sister seemed more interested in her voice mail.

"He had to help his grandpa."

Just then the familiar voice on the phone said, "You have five messages. First message 5:20 this evening."

"Message one: 'Hi, this is Ty. Uh, I'm here at your house. I see your car by the garage. I rang the bell. I knocked on the door. It doesn't seem like there is anyone home. I hear a dog barking. That must be Buster. Look… I'm kinda confused. Give me a call. What am I supposed to do? The number on this phone is 555-202-8122.'"

Now it was Katee who was confused. A puzzled look crept across her face as she listened intently.

"Second message 5:35 this evening. Message two: 'It's me again. The lady in the house next to yours just told me you got in a limo with some guy. I'm guessing that was Chaz. I thought you were good with going in my mom's car.'" There was a pause; then Ty continued, "Look, you never told me how to get to Mister Q's. I saw Chaz this morning. He gave me a map. From what I overheard some guys saying, maybe it's right. I just don't know. I'm going to follow it. But give me a call to be sure. Then I'll meet you there, okay? Later."

Katee's mouth was becoming dry. She felt very weak. She allowed herself to sit on the corner of the couch. It was like she was moving in slow motion. She could detect a note of disappointment in Ty's voice. It wasn't anger, but it added to the sick feeling that was overcoming her. Swallowing, she licked her lips trying to moisten them.

Keri was still ready to wring her sister's neck. She felt like she was being ignored; her patience growing thin. Even so, she stopped herself from pouncing. Katee was transforming before her eyes. The look of bewilderment on Katee's face turned Keri's irritation into concern.

"Katee? Are you okay?" she asked.

Third message 7:05 this evening. Message three: "Me again. I took the exit that Chaz said to take. There is no Mister Q's out this way. There is a town called Mitchell, but that is to the south. There was a truck stop and a McDonald's at the exit. The highway goes up through farmland after that, a few houses, a couple cornfields, and some pasture. I've gone five miles. No point in going any further. I guess you're not going to call me back now. It's after seven. I…uh…Maybe I'll stop at the Mickey D's. Burger and fries is better than nothing."

"Oh, my God," Katee whispered, the combination of disbelief and frustration in her voice. "He sent him to Mitchell."

Katee knew where the town of Mitchell was located, and she knew the truck stop and McDonald's. She had an aunt who lived in that town. Her vision was starting to blur as her eyes began to slowly fill with tears. She ran her fingers through her hair, clutching a fistful at the back of her head. It was no relief.

Mr. and Mrs. Roberts were slowly making their way to the living room. Keri shrugged as they exchanged glances. They would have to wait until Katee was ready to include them in a conversation.

"Fourth message 7:50 this evening. Message four: 'Just finished my sandwich and fries. It was good. Sure you're interested in knowing.'" The sarcasm in Ty's voice was now evident. "'Just wasn't what I had planned on having for supper this evening. Look, I can't believe you guys are sitting there listening to these messages and laughing your heads off, but if you are, you must be having a really boring evening. Oh, well. You know the girl behind the counter is kinda cute. Maybe I'll see if I can get her number.'"

Katee rose to her feet, wiping a tear from her eye as she did so. She heaved a heavy, labored sigh, quivering as she exhaled.

The others in the room, again exchanging glances, did not know what to say until Katee put down the phone and turned her attention to them.

"Fifth message 10:10 this evening. Message five: 'It's me again. This is the last time. I promise. I went ahead and came on home. I thought about it all the way. I think I've got it figured out now. You guys set me up. Wasn't just you, it was the whole Gang. That first time when you and Teej came over, that must have been part of it. The bus ride, you must've planned that. That's why you were there by yourself. I took the bait, I guess. Then you came to my house and reeled me in. Now as I think about it I should have picked up on a few signs. Was it because I'm the new kid? I don't understand. I could have gone to homecoming by myself or with someone else; or maybe that was the deal, keep the new kid from going to homecoming, like I shouldn't have been invited. I guess that's not important now…I do want my thirty dollars back. You can tell Chaz I will have my thirty dollars back or I'll take it out of his hide…I suppose there is nothing else to say. Pretty sure you won't be calling me now, so I'm going to shut the phone off and give it back to Mom.'"

"There are no more new messages. To replay these messages…"

Katee closed her phone. Panic overcame her as tears continued to fill her eyes. She turned to her mother with the urgency of the moment, "Mom," she pleaded. "I have to go to Ty's."

Her mother looked to her husband as she answered, "Katee, it's almost midnight."

"Dad… Please," implored Katee, her voice filled with desperation as a tear began to trickle down her cheek. "He's still up. I know he is. He's in his room, hating me. I just know it."

Her father tried to be firm yet compassionate. "It is too late. You can go see him tomorrow. It'll be okay…Why would he be hating you, anyway?"

She could not hold back the flood of tears any longer. Keri retrieved the phone from her hand. "No it won't. It won't be okay.

He will hate me. Oh God, I know he'll hate me," Katee groaned in frustration as she threw herself on the couch, burying her face in a pillow, sobbing uncontrollably.

Her mother quickly went to her side, gently rubbing her back, offering the only kind words she could think of, as she tried to comfort her. She looked to her husband. All she received in return was a shrug.

Keri knew the password to Katee's voice mail. She quickly accessed the messages.

Mother and Father waited for Keri to shed some light on what was going on. After hearing the first two messages, she said one word that pretty much explained the source of their youngest daughter's distress, "Chaz." Dad grimaced. Mom shook her head. They would all take turns listening to messages from Ty.

After some time had passed, Keri suggested that Katee call, leaving a message. Maybe Ty could hear it first thing in the morning.

Katee took the suggestion. It was at least something she could do. "Ty this is Katee. I can explain everything. I'll see you tomorrow as soon as I can. Please don't be mad at me!" Her message ended, Katee said, "I can't believe this happened. Why does Chaz have to be such a jerk?"

Keri was quick to reply, "I can't tell you why he's a jerk. But I can tell you, he certainly is a jerk. Always has been and always will be."

"Get no argument here," added their father.

Deanne glared at her husband. "You're not helping."

"Well, it's the truth," Thad said.

It was now nearly two in the morning, Keri motioned to her parents that they should go to bed. Katee was trying to sleep on the couch, still wearing the dress she had worn to homecoming. Keri rocked back in the recliner, watching her sister fall asleep. Once convinced that Katee was actually asleep, Keri allowed herself to follow suit.

Ty entered the kitchen, the smell of breakfast in the air. Trace was helping their mother. Grandpa was seated at the table nursing a cup of coffee as he read the morning paper.

"Good morning," Ty said.

"Good morning," replied his mother.

GPa mumbled, "Morning," but kept on reading.

Trace was even less cordial. "'Bout time you got up, lazy."

"Oh, yeah," said Ty. "How long have you been up?" As the words came out of his mouth, his mother turned to face her son. That is when he noticed, she was wearing the corsage from last night. Ty smiled. "Looks great on you, Mom."

"Thank you," she said, a look of satisfaction on her face. "I think it looks nice, too."

Trace had shared with both her and GPa what she had learned of the events of last night. Mom had instructed the others to not bring any of the matter up unless Ty were to do so. She placed a hand on his shoulder as she said, "After you've had some breakfast, could you go get us a gallon of milk?"

"Sure, I can do that."

"Just as well take the old truck and fill it with gas," GPa said. "I'll give you some cash."

"Okay." After breakfast, Ty drove the old pickup to the convenience store. They called it the "Old Truck" because it was the older of two pickups on the farm. GPa used it as his work vehicle. Usually, it had a couple stocks of corn growing in the back. Now was no exception.

Ty had pumped the gas, paid for it along with the gallon of milk, and was returning to the truck when Todd drove up and called to him, "Hey, Ty."

Ty responded as he put the milk into the seat on the passenger's side of the truck, "Hi, Todd. What do you know?"

"Not a lot...We missed you at Mister Q's last night. Thought you were coming with Katee?"

"Yeah...Well, that didn't work out. She was there though, I guess?" Ty glanced at Todd to see his face as he answered, as though the expression on his face might give added information.

"Sure, she was there, with Teej, Denny, and Chaz."

"They seemed to have a good time, I suppose."

"Oh, yeah...They were laughing and dancing. Al even danced with Katee. He cut in on Chaz, so he could ask where you were. I don't suppose Chaz liked it very well."

"Oh, really...So where did she say I was?"

Todd paused. "That you had to help your grandpa." The words came out slowly as if he suspected by Ty's question something wasn't right.

"I see." Ty walked around the truck and climbed in behind the wheel on the driver's side.

"You did have to help your grandpa, didn't you?" asked Todd with puzzled concern.

"Not last night," Ty answered, fidgeting as he started the truck. Then he repeated himself, "Not last night," more softly, unable to conceal the hint of disappointment.

Todd watched as Ty drove away, fishing his cell phone from his pocket then dialing. "Hey, Al. Guess what I just found out?"

It was after eleven when Katee began to wake. The world seemed to slowly come into focus. She wiped some sleep from her eyes. The tears from last night had left them red. For those first few brief moments, Katee forgot about last evening, but those memories quickly came flooding back. She jumped up as though suddenly startled. "Ty...I've got to see Ty," she said with a panicky tone.

Keri and their mother were nearby in the kitchen area; Thad was in the garage. "You'd better take a shower first. You look like crap," Keri said, offering some sisterly advice.

"And then have something to eat," her mother said. "I am not sure what you might call it. It is too late for breakfast and too early for lunch. Maybe this is the time of day for brunch."

On most Sundays, the Robertses would have been up long ago. Sometimes they would go to church services, sometimes not. Last night had taken its toll on the entire family, so the decision was made to stay home.

Katee only half heard her mother and sister as she bounded up the stairs. She would hurriedly take a shower, all the while rehearsing what she would say to Ty. Surely, he would listen. It was all Chaz's doing. He had lied to both Ty and her, for that matter to Teej and Denny as well. She talked to the mirror as she brushed and dried her hair.

Her mom was waiting for her as she came down the stairs.

"What do you want do you want to eat?"

"I'm really not hungry."

"All the more reason you have to have something to eat, at least some cereal. You are not going to the Henrys with an empty stomach."

"Okay," Katee said reluctantly. "I'll have some toast."

"Keri is going with you and she is driving."

Katee did not argue the point. "Okay… We are going in just a few minutes," Katee said stubbornly. She ate her toast, along with a glass of juice. She might have been just a little hungry, although she never would have admitted it.

It was a little after one thirty in the afternoon when Katee and Keri pulled into the Henry's driveway.

Katee took a deep breath as she unbuckled the seatbelt. Opening the door she said, "Wish me luck."

"It'll be okay," said Keri softly.

Katee walked briskly to the porch. That she felt some apprehension would be an understatement. Her stomach was tight. It felt like there was a huge knot in it. Still…she wanted to make things right so badly that she could overcome any physical discomfort, or at least so she thought. Ty would listen. He would understand. He wouldn't be mad. They would work this out. It would be okay. It just had to be.

She pressed the doorbell, stepped back, nervously waiting, hoping Ty would answer the door, still trying to think what she would say. She had it all planned. Now she couldn't remember the plan.

The door opened. It was Trace. "Oh, it's you. What do you want?" Her tone was less than friendly.

"I need to talk to Ty." She started to say, "I can expl—," but Trace cut her off.

Trace looked over her shoulder and called out, "It's that thing. Do you want to talk to her or do you want me to kick her rear?" Folding her arms, she returned a menacing stare toward Katee.

Katee tightened her lips and stiffened her stance but did not budge beyond that.

Ty responded from somewhere in the house. "Unless she has my thirty dollars, we don't need to talk… And don't bother with the other."

Still glaring, Trace started to repeat what her brother had just said, "He says he wants—"

"I'll get the thirty dollars," Katee snapped. She bounded off the porch; her face reddening with anger. She jumped back in the car with Keri. "We are going to Chaz's," she said. "He owes Ty thirty dollars."

"O…kay," said Keri.

It was only a couple of miles from the Henry farm to where the Thomases lived. The Thomas house was on a small acreage. They had a couple of dogs, but no livestock.

As the sisters drove up, they could see Chaz sprawled over the engine of a car with its hood up. Chaz's dad was in the garage entrance way, wiping his hands with a rag.

"You're calm, right," Keri asked as she stopped the car.

"You darn right I am. You'll see just how calm I am." Katee was out of the car before Keri had time to react.

Keri hurriedly followed, thinking, *This won't be good*.

Chaz righted himself from the car, seeing his visitors, he said, "Hey, ladies."

Once Katee was close enough to do so, the palm of her right hand struck Chaz flush on his left cheek, followed by the left hand, which glanced off his nose, at the same time shouting, "Liar!"

"What the heck…" Chaz raised his arms in defense and rocked back on his heels, just in time to duck another right hand. His dad rushed to intervene as did Keri.

"You're a dirty liar, and you know it," Katee shouted.

Loudly, Chaz said, "You had a good time!"

Katee yelled, "I would have had a better time with Ty! You knew I wanted to go with him!"

Mr. Thomas and Keri were trying keep them separated and establish some order.

Finally, Mr. Thomas had enough. He raised his voice. "Both of you stop it." And for some reason they did. "Now…Keri, what is this all about?"

Katee started to speak, but Keri shushed her and explained to Mr. Thomas, "Katee was to go to homecoming with Ty Henry. Chaz horned in. He told a few lies so he could go with Katee. Katee found out. Now she's mad. Ty didn't go to homecoming at all. So Chaz owes Ty thirty dollars, the cost of the meals."

Mr. Thomas sighed. Reaching for his wallet, he said, "I think I get the picture. Here is forty, keep the extra for the inconvenience. Chaz, you'll owe me… Katee, I'm sorry. I apologize for my son. That is not the way to treat friends."

Katee took the two twenty-dollar bills. "Thank you," she said, still boiling. She gave one last disgusted look toward Chaz, before turning toward the car.

Keri nodded to Mr. Thomas and gave Chaz her own admonishing look, then followed her sister.

Mr. Thomas turned to his son, "I don't need to know the details, but why would you do such a thing?"

"All's fair in love and war…right?"

"No. That's not right. And you will repay me the forty dollars."

Minutes later, Katee and Keri were back at the Henrys'. Katee clutched the forty dollars as she released the seat belt, opening the door. "Let's try this again."

Keri didn't say anything, but she made a silent wish that all would go well.

Trace answered the door again. This time Katee spoke first. "I have the money."

Trace called over her shoulder, "She's back…this time with your money. I'm going to talk to Keri."

Intentionally bumping Katee on her way out the door, Trace went to see Keri. She climbed into the passenger side of the car. "I'm not happy with your sister."

"Before you crucify her, let me tell you what happened," Keri came to the defense of her sister. She proceeded to share what she had learned of the happenings of the night before, as well as the confrontation with Chaz minutes earlier.

Ty came out onto the porch.

Katee held out the forty dollars. "I got this from Chaz's dad. He's going to make Chaz repay him."

"It was only thirty." Ty retrieved his wallet from his pocket, taking out ten dollars.

"He said you could keep the extra."

"It was thirty dollars," said Ty. "I won't be bought."

"Okay," Katee said softly, taking the change and stuffing it in her pocket. She didn't want to argue over the money. That wasn't why she was here.

Ty sat down on the porch, his long legs hanging over the steps. "You said you wanted to talk."

Katee sat down next to him. "It wasn't my fault. I wanted to go out with you last night. Teej and Denny didn't have anything to do with it either. It was all Chaz's doing. He lied to us, and he must've lied to you. This is what happened." Then she proceeded to tell the story of how the evening had unfolded.

Ty seemed to stare at the ground the whole while.

"I didn't get your messages until I got home. Almost 11:30. I felt so bad. Mom and Dad wouldn't let me come see you. I am so sorry. There's got to be some way to fix this. We could go out Saturday, and I'll pay for everything."

"Are they having another homecoming next week?"

Katee's spirits were suddenly dashed. She had hoped that Ty would have reacted differently. She was hoping he would be sympathetic toward her and angry with Chaz. "No… I guess not. There would be other things we could do though."

"Did you have fun?"

"What?" Katee was a little surprised by the question. Maybe even a little annoyed.

"Did you have fun last night with Chaz?"

Afraid she might say the wrong thing, Katee was very deliberate. "I…thought…you…were…helping your grandpa and had stood me up." She stole a glance at Ty. "So, yes, we had a good time. We all did." Then quickly added, "But it would have been better with you there, and knowing what I know now, it's all been ruined."

Ty looked out toward the car that Keri and Trace were in. "Is there anything else?"

"I deserve a second chance. We deserve a second chance."

Ty stood up. He seemed to tower over Katee. "Not today. Not today," he said again softly. Then he went back into the house.

Katee felt empty. It went the way she feared, not the way she had hoped. She felt a tear forming in her eye. She wiped it with her finger. She had cried so much the last twelve or so hours there were not a lot of tears left to be cried. She sat paralyzed for a minute, then finally stood up and walked slowly toward the car.

Trace got out and met Katee as she neared the car. "Look, I guess I was a little hard on you. I'm sorry." Katee forced a weak smile. Trace nodded to Keri then headed to the house.

Katee climbed into the car, buckled the seat belt, and put her head back against the headrest. "He hates me. He hates me, Keri."

"I doubt that he hates you."

"Yes he does," her eyes staring aimlessly. "And this hurts; it really hurts. I feel like I did something dirty." Her voice was shaky and cracked as she spoke, the frustration clearly visible.

"I know," Keri said softly. She reached over and took her sister's hand. "I know. Look… You didn't do anything dirty. It wasn't your fault. You didn't do anything wrong. You're hurting because you've got a love'n heart. You care. You care how other people feel and how they feel about you. And from what Trace tells me, so does Ty. So let the dust settle and give things a chance to work out. Don't give up, not yet. Okay?"

"Okay," answered Katee weakly. "Okay."

Chapter Six

As Keri and Katee pulled into the Robertses' drive, the door to the house opened, and out walked Teej. The look on her face was somber, much like the expression on Katee's face.

"How did it go?" Teej asked after Katee got out of the car and walked toward her, along with Keri.

"Not so good," Katee answered, an unmistakable sadness in her voice.

Teej wrapped her arms around her best friend with a comforting hug.

"He hates me, Teej. He hates all of us."

"Oh, K. Did he say that?"

"He didn't have to." She pulled away from her friend's embrace. "What all do you know?"

"Denny called me. Said he had heard that Ty wasn't helping his grandpa and that I should talk to you to see what was up. Then your mom filled me in with what she knew."

"Let's go upstairs, and I'll tell you the rest."

Mrs. Roberts watched as the girls came through the door. Katee and Teej went directly to the stairway leading to the second floor and Katee's room. She looked to Keri for a sign. Keri returned the look with a shake of her head. The news would not be that all is well.

Teej and Katee would spend the next couple of hours in Katee's room. Teej listened to the voice messages that Ty had left. There were a lot of "Oh my God" and "Chaz is such a jerk."

Teej laughed when Katee told the story of how she had slapped Chaz. "You should have hit him with a two by four."

"I might have, if there would have been one handy." Katee flopped to her back on her bed, staring at the ceiling. "I can't believe this happened. Why did it have to happen?"

"I don't know, K."

"I just wanted to go to homecoming with Ty. I like him. And he liked me, before this all happened. Teej, when we talk, when I'm around Ty, I feel confident. Oh, I don't know how to describe it. I just wanted to get to know him and for him to know me."

"I know what you mean. I can see it, whenever you talk about him or look at him."

"Am I really that obvious?"

"Come on. We're best friends…forever…remember? You knew when I first started liking Denny."

"Speaking of which, how did he find out about all of this? You said he called you."

"He said he heard it from Al. Everyone at Hillcrest probably knows what happened by now."

Teej wasn't too far off. Todd had started the ball rolling by telling Al, who then told three others who told three others and so on. Once the first domino fell, the others followed. That doesn't mean anyone had the complete or accurate story. Nonetheless, the story was told. By Monday morning, it would be the talk of Hillcrest High.

Teej called Denny later Sunday evening to fill him in on the details.

On Monday morning, Denny drove to Chaz's house before going on to school.

Chaz came out to meet him. "Hey, Bud. What's up?"

"What were you thinking?" Denny had stewed all Sunday night. He decided, after a restless night of sleep, he would confront Chaz.

"What do mean?" Chaz tried to act innocent.

"You know what I'm talking about. You lied about Ty. Geez, you lied to all of us. Did you think Katee wouldn't find out? That everyone wouldn't find out?" There was a certain futility in

Denny's manner. A frustration with the realization that he had been an unwilling party to something he found to be wrong.

"Like you said, the early bird gets the worm. Well, I got the worm."

"You moron; you lied to friends. That's not how you treat friends." Denny's frustration was now showing signs of anger. "You did this to the 'Team.' You can't be that stupid."

"Yeah, well that dork's not good enough to go with Katee. We don't need him cutting in."

"You've got to be kidding." Denny threw up his hands. "You are such an idiot." He turned to go back to his car. "You had better be ready for practice tonight."

"The dork won't do anything," said Chaz.

"Oh really, well, what about Al? He's ticked off, too. And so are some other guys." Denny slammed his car door as he called back to Chaz, "You'd better'd wear your cup to practice… Buddy. It could get rough." Then he peeled out.

Chaz smirked, "Yeah, yeah." Inside though, Chaz was beginning to question his own actions last Saturday night. He hadn't counted on alienating so many people. In fact, he had hoped to win Katee over. That didn't seem to have worked so well, at least not if Sunday had proved any indication.

The first bell rang. Katee was at her locker with Teej.

Carrie Jones and Tess Marion were passing in the hall. They were seniors, not really friends of Teej and Katee, but not bitter enemies or anything. Slight rivals maybe.

"Hey, Katee, heard what you did to Ty. That was pretty crappy." Tess was first to speak.

"Yeah," added Carrie. "I would've gone with him."

Katee bristled, clenching her teeth. Fortunately, Teej stepped between Katee and the two girls before Katee was able to react any further.

"It wasn't Katee's fault. Chaz is the one who caused it all."

Katee turned back to her locker, while Teej explained what had happened Saturday night. "She feels awful, so give her some space…please." She added the "please" hoping it might appeal to the girls' sense of fairness.

After the two girls had left, Katee slammed her locker shut. "It's going to be like this all day, isn't it?"

"Well, I'm going to be with you all day. It'll be okay. When everyone hears what happened, they'll understand it wasn't your fault."

At that moment, Ty happened to walk past the girls. He did not speak. He just steadfastly moved on his way.

Katee unknowingly held her breath as he walked by. After he had passed, she said, "He didn't even look at me." She shook her head slightly. "God!" She hit her locker, oblivious to the stares of others in the vicinity.

It felt like the longest day ever. Katee was miserable. Surely, everyone was talking about her.

Ty never did talk to her that day. In fact, he seemed to go out of his way to avoid her.

True, Katee was not directly to blame for what had happened. Even so, neither was Ty. He probably had every right to feel the way he did: betrayed, angry, taken advantage of, deceived, humiliated maybe. He certainly was not about to be understanding or forgiving—not today.

Mercifully, the last class of the day ended. After a quick stop at her locker, Katee went straight to her car. Teej was close by her side. Teej had rode with her this morning, so she would ride home with her this afternoon.

"Well, I guess we got through it," Teej said lightheartedly. Getting no reaction from Katee, she added, "You're going to be okay, right?"

"I suppose," said Katee. "Don't have much of a choice, do I?"

"No…not really," said Teej. "Give it time."

"I don't want to give it time. Why did we have to be so stupid? Why was I so dumb? All I had to have done was to wait for Ty. He showed up at 5:30 just like he said he was going to, then, I would have known Chaz was lying. Why were we so dumb as to believe we weren't allowed to have our cells? If we had kept our phones, I would've gotten Ty's message. God!" She gripped the wheel harder. They pulled into Teej's drive.

"I guess we were all pretty dumb. Dumb to trust a friend," Teej said.

"Some friend; you don't even like him. I don't like him very much right now."

"Maybe things will be better tomorrow," Teej said softly.

"We can only hope. I don't see how they could get any worse," Katee said sarcastically.

"You want to come in for a while?"

"No, I don't think so. I just want to go home and…I don't know, scream or break something. I don't know what I want to do. Maybe, just be alone for a while."

"Okay," Teej said understandingly. "But call me if you need me; if you want to talk or anything."

"Yeah, I will." Katee choked on her words ever so slightly.

The day for Ty wasn't a whole lot better. He went out of his way to avoid Katee, but that didn't mean that he didn't think about her and what had happened. For him it was a little different though. Generally speaking, the word around school was that he got the shaft. As a result, he received a great deal of sympathy. Todd caught him at his locker.

"Hey, I heard what really happened Saturday. That really sucks."

"Yeah…Well it's over." Ty tried to take the high road.

"What are you going to do? You can't let that big mouth get away with this. I'll back you up. I bet the whole team will."

"We're making a run for the playoffs. Just let it go."

Todd seemed frustrated by Ty's response. "Ty…the guy is a jerk. He needs to get taken down. Don't let this slide."

"I don't know that it's worth it. I don't know that it was all his doing." Ty shook his head slightly, "I just don't know, okay." Then he went on his way.

Todd was a little irritated. He said, apparently talking to himself, "Chaz is gonna take some hits tonight. Whether you are in on it or not, Buddy."

Later in the day, Ty was at lunch sitting by himself. He could see Katee and Teej across the room. He pretended not to notice when Katee would glance his direction. He tried to focus on his lunch, although he wasn't really that hungry.

Suddenly, his thoughts were interrupted by visitors—Chaz and a friend of Chaz's: Lance Lawrence, a junior and Chaz wannabe.

"Hey guy," Chaz broke into Ty's thoughts. "How's it going?"

"Ah…Could be better, could be worse. Thanks for asking." There was a subtle hint of sarcasm in Ty's voice that was probably wasted on Chaz.

"So, I heard you went all the way to Mitchell. That was just a joke, you understand. No hard feelings." Chaz extended his hand to shake hands with Ty. He had that smirky look.

"You know," Ty began. Out of the corner of his eye, he could see Katee was watching. "There may be a few hard feelings. So, how about you go on your way, and I'll finish my lunch."

Incredulous, Chaz had a look of disbelief. After all, he had offered his hand; Ty had refused to shake it. It is likely that Ty would rather break Chaz's hand off than shake it. Chaz may not have understood that. As he turned away from Ty, he saw Katee. Chaz shrugged.

Katee just turned away, trying to be invisible.

Ty had a doctor's appointment right after school. Nothing serious. He smacked a helmet in Friday night's game, jamming a finger on his left hand; the coaches wanted him to get it looked at. It actually felt better today than it did on Saturday morning. Still, coach had said get it checked out. He wanted his star receiver ready for the next game or at least the following one if he had to sit one out. It would mean that Ty would be late to practice. On this day, that really didn't hurt Ty's feelings any.

The guys were in the locker room getting ready for practice. Chaz was describing how he had manipulated his way into what he described as a "date with Katee Roberts," outmaneuvering his competition. An end-around, he called it. His audience consisted of Lance, a sophomore, and two freshmen. They seemed impressed by the story, although one of the freshmen had his doubts.

Al was nearby. He heard the talk, the boasting and the laughter, none of which was sitting well with him. If Ty wasn't going to get angry about this, Al was. He grabbed his helmet. As he walked past Chaz, he banged into him, throwing Chaz into the lockers.

Chaz bristled. "Hey, watch it."

Al stopped and with a sober look replied, "Excuse me," then headed on out to the field.

The team went through the usual warm up and stretching drills. It was a normal practice. Coach had a couple of new plays he wanted to use in this week's game. He always tried to bring in a couple of new plays each week. He thought that helped to keep the team fresh and focused; so he told his assistants. Perhaps this season that was more important than in seasons past. Hillcrest was two games away from making the playoffs. Essentially, win and they were in. So there was a bit of a buzz around school at the possibility of making the playoffs. Nothing was being taken for granted, however.

The coach was Albert Gray, a sixteen-year veteran. He had reached the playoffs with teams four times, advancing to the quarterfinals on two of those occasions. He was a dedicated coach, but a teacher first. Teaching was a passion. Football provided him a topic. Make no mistake, Coach Gray enjoyed the game of football and he liked to win, but it was what kids learned from playing the game that provided him the greatest reward.

Coach Gray had diagrammed a play, explaining it in detail to his players. Now was time for them to run the play…all a matter of routine, or so Coach Gray expected.

Chaz took his place under center. He wore an orange jersey. All of the quarterbacks wore orange jerseys. The jerseys made them easily recognizable. Defensive players were to not make contact with any player wearing an orange jersey. The coaches did not want key players accidentally injured in practice, especially not this time of the season.

Al took his place on the defensive side of the ball. A freshman was assigned to block him. The play was designed to go the opposite direction. The thinking being that for this play, Al's side of the defense would not be involved. All that the freshman had to do was step in front of the player on defense, in this case Al. That would be "Big Al." Division I football recruit Al, the same Al who was upset with the stunt that Chaz had pulled on Ty and Katee.

Al looked at the freshman, shaking his head slightly. His gaze alone was enough to strike terror in a player of comparable ability. The freshman swallowed hard, taking his stance. There was no place to hide; retreat seemed to be the better part of valor in this instance.

Chaz barked out the signals with his usual air of confidence. Al exploded from his position. You would have thought the playoffs were at stake with this very play. The freshman barely brushed him as Al blew by him. Chaz had dropped back to pass. He wasn't concerned with a rush from Al's side of the line. After all, Chaz wore the orange jersey. His lack of concern changed abruptly as he felt two huge arms wrap around his torso. The ball went flying from Chaz's grasp. Chaz learned firsthand what it was like to be tackled by the All-Stater. Surely, he had been hit by Al before, perhaps not when Al was quite as motivated as he was today. Al drove Chaz into the ground. He wanted to make sure Chaz felt it…and he did.

Coach Gray almost swallowed his whistle before exclaiming in disbelief, "What the …?" He then rushed to his quarterback.

"My bad, coach," Al said. He fully expected to be chastised for laying a lick on the quarterback.

Coach Gray glared at Al. "You know better."

Meanwhile, Chaz groaned as his wind slowly returned. Finally, he sat up and was helped to his feet.

"Walk it off. You'll be okay in a minute."

Easy for Coach to say, thought Chaz.

"Okay, I'm ready," Chaz said at last.

"Are you sure?" the coach asked.

"Yeah, yeah…let's do it again." Chaz took his position as did the other players. He began to call the signals, taking a glance toward Al. As the ball was snapped, Chaz dropped back to pass, stealing another look at Al. This time the rush came from his right. It was an inspired Todd who slipped past a would-be blocker. He jumped the count by a beat, so the blocker did not have a chance. Neither did Chaz. Todd drilled him pretty hard—although not with anything near the impact that Al administered—driving Chaz to the turf with some authority.

This time Chaz held on to the ball and didn't loose his breath.

"You idiot! What are you doing?" Chaz shouted, throwing the ball at Todd as Todd stood up.

"There's only one idiot on this team, and I'm looking at him." Todd retaliated, kicking Chaz's leg.

"Knock it off!" Coach Gray said sternly, as he rushed to intervene.

Chaz was on his feet as the coaches and other players separated Todd and Chaz. The usual epithets being slung at one another; the "bulldogs" were growling. No punches were actually thrown, but there were a few shoves.

"What's this all about?" Coach Gray said, regaining some control. Suddenly, no one had anything to say, although a few grunted. "Okay, seniors to the bleachers."

The bleachers are where the coach took players to have heart to heart talks. It was kind of the "whipping shed." Not that the players were gathered there only for negative talks, but most could tell in this case the coach was not happy.

Coach Gray instructed one of his assistants to continue working with the rest of the team, while he and another assistant, Jed Thompson, followed the five seniors to the bleachers.

"So let's hear it. What's going on?" the coach asked. No one said a word. "There is something," said the coach.

Finally, Al broke the silence. "Coach…you were at homecoming at Mister Q's on Saturday night. Did you see Ty there?"

Coach Gray thought for a moment, then answered, "No, I don't think I did. But then again…"

"That's because he wasn't there. Chaz can tell you why." Al gave a stern look toward Chaz.

"Okay…Coach," Coach Gray gestured to Coach Thompson. Then he instructed, "You and Chaz go for a walk. Find out his side of the story. And the rest of you are going to tell me the other side."

Chaz slammed his helmet against the front row of the bleachers then followed Coach Thompson.

As soon as Chaz and Coach Thompson were out of ear shot, "Details, gentlemen. And let's stop beating around the bush."

"Denny. Tell him what happened," Al said. "You know better than any of the rest of us."

Denny took a deep breath, quivering as he did so. He clutched the face mask of his helmet and stared at the ground to help maintain his composure. "Ty was supposed to go with Katee. Chaz horned in. He lied to Katee. He lied to me and Teej. He lied to Ty."

"Ty is one of us," blurted out Todd. "Chaz did this to the team." There seemed to be agreement all around; the facial expressions of the four seniors made that very evident.

"Okay, so exactly what did Chaz do? Tell me what happened," Coach Gray said firmly.

Denny then told the story of the evening.

Patiently, Coach Gray listened, careful to not react, although admittedly this was a first.

"That pretty much is it, Coach. Katee checked her phone after she got home. Ty had been trying to call her. He left her voice messages. That's when she first found out that we had been played," Denny said.

"I saw Ty uptown, Sunday morning. That's when I knew something wasn't right," added Todd.

"Okay, I need to think about this. Anyone have anything else to say?"

"He can't get away with it, Coach." Al shook his head as he spoke. "He can't get away with it. He can't do that to 'Team.' It's low rent, regardless. But it's worse when you do it to 'Team.'"

Coach Gray looked at the four seniors. Now their body language spoke volumes, and the message was clear. This is when a coach truly earns his money. "Okay. We will talk about this some more. I need to hear from Chaz. You guys get back to practice."

As the four rejoined the team, Coach Gray motioned for Coach Thompson to join him and for Chaz to remain where he was. As Jed approached, Coach Gray asked, "Are you sure you want to become a head coach someday?"

Jed chuckled, shaking his head. "Makes a person think."

"So what did he tell you?"

"Oh, he didn't do anything wrong. All's fair in love and war. She's too good for Ty. He tried to square things with Ty, but he wouldn't shake hands with him. Yadda, yadda, yadda. How about the others? What did they think?"

"You saw the hits by Al and Todd. That pretty well sums up their feelings." Coach Gray rubbed his hand over his jaw thoughtfully. "I think we'll send Chaz home. I don't know exactly how to handle this. This is one for the books. Let's make sure Jack gets plenty of reps." That would be Jack North, the backup quarterback.

Coach Gray walked toward where Chaz was waiting. "Anything you want to tell me?"

"Just that this is a bunch of crap," Chaz said indignantly.

"How so?"

"The orange jersey… You don't hit the guy wearing the orange jersey."

"Yep…It's hands off the player with the orange jersey, gotta be awfully upset to break that rule. Might want to think about why they are so upset. I think you know. For now, go ahead and hit the showers. We'll talk in the morning."

"This is all a bunch of crap."

"Yeah, I know. We will talk in the morning, my office, 8 a.m. Tell your dad, I'll call him tonight…about 8:30."

"Whatever."

Chaz strode past the team, glancing over his shoulder at the players, still defiant, certain he had been wronged. As he entered the locker room, he found Ty lacing his shoes. He gave him a disgusted looked.

Ty mostly ignored Chaz. However, as Ty stood, closing his locker, he couldn't help but look Chaz's way.

"What are you looking at?" asked Chaz.

"Nothing in particular," Ty said. "Practice over?"

"Is for me. I may be done for the year."

"Oh." Ty nodded, not really understanding.

With helmet in hand, Ty left Chaz to wallow in his own self pity. Once out of the building, he broke into a jog toward the field. On the sidelines, he started his usual routine of stretches.

Coach Thompson was the first to take notice of Ty's arrival. "What'd they say?"

"Just jammed...nothing broken. He said to tape it for a couple of practices and it'll be good." Ty held up the injured hand so Coach could see the tape job.

"So you are good to catch some balls?"

"Yep...It doesn't feel bad today." Ty might have fudged a bit on that, but true it was feeling a lot better than it had earlier.

"Good. We need you catching some passes from Jack."

"Okay." Ty looked toward the field where Jack was calling plays with the first team. After factoring in the comment from Chaz minutes earlier, this could only mean that Jack would be the quarterback for Friday's game, so Ty deduced.

Practice would last another forty-five minutes or so. Coach Gray called the team together. He had them sit on the ground while he went over some informational items. Finally, he was ready to release the players.

"One last thing, we will talk about this other matter tomorrow. I will let you know then what is going to happen. We are two games away from the playoffs. But make no mistake about it. I care more about this sport...and...this team, in that order, than I do about making the playoffs." He emphasized his words so as to make an impression. "I will tell you what is going to happen; then you can decide what you want to do. I'd like Jack and the receivers and the two centers to stay a little longer. If you have to go, then go. The rest of you; hit the showers."

"I want you guys running a few more routes," the coach said to the players he had asked to stay. And they did stay. In fact, so did the entire offensive and defensive lines. They said they wanted more work coming off the ball. The guys on defense said they would try to make Jack more uncomfortable, so he could get a better feel for what it felt like to play varsity quarterback. Coach did not argue. They all worked another half an hour.

Ty didn't give a lot of thought to the coach's parting comments. Nor did anyone have anything much to say in the locker room. He was more interested in getting home than anything else. Although he was more convinced now than before that Jack would be the QB on Friday. Or maybe the coach wanted Ty to get in some extra practice since he had been late. No matter. He was sure the coach had his reasons. If he wanted the team to know, he would fill them in.

The next morning, Chaz reported to Coach Gray's office as he had been instructed to do. The phone call his father received the night before made missing the appointment not an option. Chaz's dad had spoken with him, in total agreement with Coach Gray. The possibility of losing the use of a car took some of the arrogance out of Chaz's sails, at least temporarily.

The door to the coach's office was open, so Chaz knocked on the door frame "Hey, Coach."

"Chaz…come on in…close the door," Coach Gray instructed. Chaz complied.

"I guess your dad laid it out for you."

"Yeah." Chaz nodded.

"So you tell me. What's your plan?"

"I want to finish the season. I want to be part of the team."

"Okay. That means you'll sit on Friday. I am not going to preach to you. You have probably heard enough of that already. What I am going to tell you though, is that you need to regain some trust. I think you lost it from your teammates. As a quarterback, you can't have that. We can't have that. You have to be the leader. That means you need the team's respect. You lost some of that."

"I tried to apologize to Ty. I offered to shake hands on it. He wouldn't take it."

"Well…he was probably a little bent out of shape, too. Regardless, you've got some fences to mend. We'll have a team meeting before practice. You'll get to talk to the team then. Okay?"

"Yeah. Sure. Thanks, Coach."

Chaz left the coach's office, seemingly more contrite, humble, maybe even a better person than he had been twenty-four hours earlier.

Later in the day, Coach Gray had the opportunity to talk to Ty. He called him in from his PE class.

Coach led Ty into his office. "Grab a chair. This will only take a minute."

Ty wasn't sure what the coach wanted to talk about; however, he was pretty sure he hadn't done anything wrong. He picked a chair, one of two available to choose from and neither looking all that comfortable to sit in.

"I heard you had some problems on Saturday making it to Mister Q's."

Ty became a little uneasy. This wasn't something he wanted to discuss with an adult, let alone his football coach. Ty respected Coach Gray, but they had known each other for only a few months. Hardly long enough to feel as though he could confide in him. Why should he? There were things Ty wouldn't want to talk to his own mother about, this being one of them. He wiped a drop of sweat from his brow, likely the result of moving from the gym to the coach's office, then readied himself to respond to the coach.

"And that Chaz had something to do with it," Coach continued. "Are you two good with each other, now?"

"Ah," Ty hesitated. "I doubt…that I will ever be good with Chaz." The words came out slow and deliberate.

"He said he apologized. Tried to shake on it and you refused. I was always taught that when a man offers his hand, the manly thing to do is to accept it."

Ty stiffened his posture, took a deep breath, then looking Coach Gray squarely in the eye, answered, "My dad always said, 'the measure of a man is not what he says but what he does, how he acts, and how he treats others.' My word matters; my handshake means something. Chaz said it was a joke. I didn't laugh. He doesn't deserve my handshake on this."

Coach Gray paused before saying, "Fair enough." He saw the conviction and maturity in Ty's words and demeanor. He saw a young man who knew what he stood for. "We are going to have a team meeting before practice. I'm hoping we can put a few things to rest and still play football. I know you'll do your job on the field. And, I do wish none of this would have happened. You should have been able to have been there Saturday night…guess you should get back to class."

"Thanks, Coach." Ty stood and left the office. He hoped the coach understood where he was coming from because one thing was certain—he had no intention of wavering on the matter.

After school the players were greeted with a sign on the locker room door: Team meeting—Get dressed and wait in the locker room. On a normal practice day players would dress and go on down to the field where they would find one of the assistants. They would then start to warm up on their own, light jogging, a little catch with a football, until the entire team and coaching staff arrived. Then Coach Gray would command, "Okay, let's get it going," and practice would officially begin.

The guys had an idea of the subject matter of this meeting. They figured it was to take place in the locker room so the public would be less likely to hear. Once in a while, parents would stop by to watch practice. Perhaps, it was fortunate that no one was watching last night's eruption. Regardless, this was likely to be the kind of team meeting that was not that pleasant. There was not a lot of the usual locker room chatter. No laughter, no boyish pranks. Rather, there was a quiet, an eerie sort of calm over the room.

Not even Chaz had anything to say. He pulled on his jersey while sitting on a bench, then propped his back against his locker.

Finally, the coach, flanked by his assistants, appeared.

"I plan on this being short and to the point," Coach Gray began; his voice commanding the attention of all of the players. He held up an orange jersey. "This is an orange jersey. Nobody hits the player wearing an orange jersey. That's been a rule since day one. Al…Todd…You broke that rule. Friday night, you sit the first quarter. Karl and Randy, you both are starting. Any questions?"

Todd and Al both nodded.

"Okay then," he continued. "Chaz, you upset this team. For that you're suspended for Friday night's game. It is up to you to square things with your teammates. Jack, you are starting QB, Friday. Make sure you are ready to go."

The players started to squirm a bit. One of Jack's close friends secretly flashed him a thumbs up, while others gave subtle glances and nods of approval of the coach's dispensation of justice. The absence of three starting seniors for the first quarter of the game had a few players concerned—given the importance of the game.

"All right, if there are no questions," Coach Gray said, "Chaz has a few things he wants to say to the team. Coach Thompson will stay in here. That is a school rule. The rest of the staff and I are going down to the field. When you get done here, anyone who still wants to play football, that's where we will be. Enough said. Floor is yours, Chaz." Coach gestured to his assistants and left the locker room.

Coach Thompson stayed behind, taking a seat out of the way. Players had to be supervised at all times. Although the rule was often bent, Coach Gray felt in this case, it was best to have someone in the room with the players to prevent any rioting that might occur.

Chaz rose to his feet, clearing his throat. "I just want to say I'm sorry. I pulled a dirty trick. I thought…I…I guess I wasn't thinking. I want to be a part of this team." He swallowed hard and cleared his throat again, trying to maintain his composure. First he looked toward Denny, then Todd and Al, and finally at Ty. "I'm sorry guys. I messed up."

The room had an uncomfortable silence. It seemed to last for minutes with no end in sight.

Ty remembered his father's words, "The measure of a man is not what he says but what he does, how he acts, and how he treats others." He would also say, "Never trust a snake." The whole time, Ty had fiddled with his helmet.

Chaz repeated himself, "I'm really sorry."

"We hear you, Chaz," Ty was the first to break the team's silence. He slapped his helmet. "Let's go play football."

A chorus from the others followed. Now some of the underclassmen gathered around Chaz, mostly the wannabes. The rest just wanted to go play, to get out of the locker room and away from the drama.

Mercifully, Friday would arrive. For the football team, the game was a needed diversion to help put to rest the prior week. Hillcrest would fall behind early. Starting jitters took a toll on the young quarterback as he threw an errant pass that was returned for a touchdown. The second quarter would start and the presence of Al and Todd in the lineup had a calming effect. Hillcrest would settle down. Ty would catch a touchdown pass tying the game. From then on, the game was never in doubt as Hillcrest would improve its record to seven and one with one game remaining. The replacements proved more than adequate.

There was a buzz in the stands. Why didn't Al and Todd start? Why didn't Chaz play? Were they injured? Would they be ready for the game next week?

And Katee, she didn't go to the game. She stayed home and watched an old movie with her mom and dad. Nope, she didn't go to the game, but she was sure glad it was Friday.

Chapter Seven

It was shortly after one o'clock Saturday afternoon. Things were pretty quiet at both the Henrys and the Robertses. It was a nice fall day. Deanne and Thad Roberts went on a shopping excursion. Mary Henry was working at the hospital, and GPa went to a farm sale. Meanwhile, the kids were all home.

Keri was doing school work at the dining room table, while Katee was reading in the living room. At the Henry house, the roles were reversed. Trace was reading, and it was Ty doing school work.

Keri decided she needed to give Trace a call. "Hey, girl. What's happening?"

"Not a lot," Trace answered.

"Did you get your accounting done?"

"Yep, did that this morning."

"Overachiever."

"Yeah…right. Had to do something," Trace said with a hint of sarcasm. "It is not exactly a hot bed of excitement over here, if you know what I mean?"

"Kinda like here, I guess. No one smiles, no one laughs. Kinda like a morgue."

Katee could feel she was being talked about. She turned, looking over her shoulder so she could see Keri. Sure enough, her sister was looking back. Katee made a face, stuck out her tongue, then turned back to the magazine she was reading.

Keri gave her a sisterly frown in return, then informed Trace, "She just made a face at me…Yeah, stuck out her tongue and everything. I wish those two would either decide they like each other or hate each other and get over it."

Katee gave an exasperated gasp and continued looking at her magazine, roughly turning a page.

"That would make our lives easier," said Trace.

"So why is Ty still mad at Katee? He has to know it was all Chaz's fault. She can't help it if she's gullible."

Hearing this part of the conversation, Katee spun herself around on the couch so she could face Keri. She was now sitting upright with both knees on the couch, rolling the magazine into a club. Her lips clenched, she wanted to say "butt out," yet was unable to bring herself to do so.

Unaware of Katee's latest contortions, Trace said, "I don't know. I'll investigate and get back to you."

"I'll keep the phone close. Later." Keri hung up, then said to Katee, "She'll get back to us."

Katee gasped, saying something that sounded like, "Grrrrrrrr." She flopped on the couch, grabbing a nearby pillow; she used it to cover her head. "Why did I have to have an older sister?"

"Oh, you love me," Keri said as she returned to her accounting.

At the Henry's house, Trace glanced at her brother across the room. Unlike Katee, Ty had been too deep in thought to pay any attention to Trace's phone conversation. Trace sauntered toward the kitchen area where he was working, books and papers spread out on the dining table.

"So, are you making any sense out of that stuff?"

"Yep," Ty replied, not raising his eyes from his work.

"Is it very hard?"

"Nope."

"Got very much to do?"

"Yep."

"Sure aren't very talkative."

"Nope."

"Can I ask you a question?"

Ty looked up from his work. "Isn't that what you've been doing, asking questions?"

"Yeah, but I mean one that you'll give a straight and complete answer to, not just yep or nope."

"Okay," Ty said, laying down his pencil. "What's on your mind?"

Trace pulled up a chair on the opposite side of the table. "You've been acting awfully cranky or at least not yourself. I know it all has to do with last weekend. What I don't get, is, why are you letting it continue? You know it was all Chaz's doing. You guys all got suckered into it. You can't be blaming Katee, can you? Why continue to be miserable?"

Ty took a deep breath, then looked away. "It's not a matter of blaming her."

"Okay, then what is it? Keri says Katee is just as miserable as you are."

Ty thought for a moment before looking back at Trace. "Let's do this. Pretend you are Katee and I'm still me. We talked about and made all of the arrangements to go to this big dance. I am to pick you up at 5:30. It is now 5 p.m. Chaz, who you have to know is not one of my friends, knocks on your door, tells you I called… him…to tell you that I am not coming… What do you do?"

"Well, first thing, I get mad, then I ca…" She stopped midsentence. It was like a light bulb came on.

"Exactly…she trusted him, not me. She didn't get mad at me. She just jumped in the car with Chaz and believed everything he told her. She didn't stop to think that I wouldn't pull something like that."

"Okay," Trace said slowly and softly. "I see where you are coming from. Do you think the way you are handling this is the best way?"

"I don't know. I don't have Dad to ask, and I'm sure not going to ask GPa or Mom." He picked up the pencil. "I need to get this done."

Trace stood up, shoving her hands into the hip pockets of her jeans. "Okay," she sighed. "I get it." She walked slowly toward the front door.

"Hey," Ty called to her just as she reached the door, causing Trace to stop and turn back his direction. "I can't ask you, either, cause you are too close to the Robertses. It would be like asking for advice from the enemy." He grinned slightly.

"Thanks a lot." She laughed and continued outside.

Minutes later, Trace was at the Robertses' front door, ringing the doorbell.

"Entrée," said Keri, trying to sound dignified.

"Why didn't you just say come in?" Katee said, shaking her head, slightly annoyed with her elder sibling.

Trace opened the door and entered the house, "Hi."

"See, she knew what I meant," Keri smugly said, before acknowledging Trace. "Hey, Trace."

Noticing Katee on the couch, Trace made sure to not leave her out. "Hi, Katee. How's it going?"

Katee replied, her back still to Trace and Keri, raising her right arm, waving her hand, and saying weakly, "Hi…and okay, I guess."

Trace looked to Keri who made a face like "That is the way she has been all week."

Trace nodded, apparently understanding the unspoken communication. Joining Keri at the table where she had been working, Trace said, "Well, I think I know what Ty's problem is."

Katee perked up, sitting a little more upright on the couch, turning her head slightly toward the two older girls in order to better eavesdrop on their conversation. She held a magazine in front of her face, still pretending to read.

Keri mouthed without speaking aloud, "She's listening," then for Katee's benefit, "Oh really. So what did you find out?"

"Well, he's not really mad at Katee. He is mad…because he thinks Katee should have gotten mad at him and called to chew him out, if she thought he'd stood her up."

"What!" Katee exploded, standing abruptly up, throwing the magazine to the floor, and turning to face Trace and Keri. "I…was…mad. And I was going to call Ty, but I didn't have a number. Chaz said we had to go right then and Ty was going to meet us at Mister Q's. That's why I didn't do anything…just ask Teej." Katee's frustration was borderline anger.

"Okay," said Keri, trying to show some calm. "You are barking at the wrong people though. You should be talking to Ty."

"I'm not barking," said Katee. "I am just good and irritated. Is Ty still at your place?"

"Yeah…at least he was when I left a little bit ago. He was doing math," Trace said humbly.

"Good." Katee's tone was firm, like she was intent on resolving matters. She grabbed her purse and stormed toward the front door. Suddenly she stopped, remembering something, and turned and ran up the stairs.

Trace looked to Keri for explanation, but received only a shrug in reply.

Moments later, Katee came back down the stairs carrying her book bag. "I'm going to see Ty. This time he's going to listen."

Katee was out the door before either Trace or Keri dare move a muscle. "So what do you think," Keri said at last, "will Ty listen?"

"I don't know." This time it was Trace who shrugged. "He can be just as stubborn as she can. But she looked awfully determined."

Katee's mind raced as she drove the short distance to the Henry farm. She rehearsed exactly what she was going to say. Problem was, the closer she got, the less sure of herself she became. Pulling into the drive, she could feel the knot in her stomach growing. She clenched her lips tightly together. *Breathe. You can do this*, she thought as she put the car into park and turned off the ignition. *He is going to listen or…or…I'll wring his neck.* Grabbing her bag, she opened the car door and slid out. Closing the door behind her with authority, she told herself again, *I can do this*. Her eyes fixated on the door; the closer she got the weaker she felt. She wanted to throw up, to turn and run. *No. No. We are going to settle this*. Now she stood on the porch. She paused for a moment, hesitating, summoning once again the courage which had deserted her, then pushed the doorbell.

Within moments, the door opened, it was Ty. There was an awkward pause before Ty offered a greeting, "Uh, hi."

Katee clutched the strap on her book bag as she replied, "Hi. Uh, Trace said you were working on math." She turned her eyes away from Ty as she told a little fib. "I need some help. I don't understand this orthogonal stuff," she said, then looked back at him.

"That just means they are perpendicular," he said, trying to be nonchalant and not condescending. "But sure, come on in. We can take a look."

Ty led the way. Katee followed. He cleared some of his papers from the table to make room for Katee.

This was the first time Katee had actually been in the Henrys' house. For some odd reason, she felt a sense of comfort as she made a quick survey of the room, perhaps because Ty had invited her in and didn't slam the door in her face. It was progress. The hard part was still to come.

Ty helped her with a chair. Meekly, Katee said, "Thank you… You have a nice house."

"Thanks. I don't do any of the decorating," Ty tried to ease some of the tension. "So, what don't you understand?"

"Oh…I don't get the dot product," Katee stammered a bit, another little fib. She hadn't rehearsed this part of the meeting, an oversight on her part. "I don't get why they are equal to zero."

"Well, they are not always equal to zero," Ty started to explain.

The knot in Katee's stomach was now starting to dissolve. A warm feeling came over her. Just being there, speaking without any angst, made her feel better. She stole a glance at Ty as he reminded her of the basics of vectors. Maybe she shouldn't bring up the real reason for her coming. Any chance they could just forget about last weekend and move on as if it never happened? Naw…probably not.

"Oh…say, did you guys win last night?" Katee asked, searching for a way to bring up her real reason for being there.

"Yeah, we came out on top. Started slow, but then things started going our way… So, let's see, dot products." Ty moved the topic back toward math.

"There is something else I need to get out," Katee interrupted, as Ty was beginning to explain how slope was related to the dot product.

Ty stopped midthought, uncertain where Katee was going next.

"Last Saturday, when I thought you had stood me up, I got mad. Teej and I talked about what you would have to do to get out of the dog house. Then, when I found out what had really happened…I was even madder, just not at you." Her hands trembled nervously as she clutched the pencil she was using. She focused on the pencil, concentrating. "There has to be something, some way that I can make things right. I know you missed out on homecoming and you can't get that back, but we could go somewhere else." Now her voice quivered, ever so slightly.

There it was again, that deafening silence. It seemed to last an eternity. It always does.

Ty looked around the room, as if searching for an answer. After a long pause, he said, "Pie."

"What?" said Katee, not quite understanding, yet feeling relieved that he had said something.

"Pie…banana cream pie. And you have to make it."

"Okay," she said, sitting more upright in her chair as if accepting a challenge. "Can I have help?"

"You can have help, but you have to make it. None of that store bought stuff."

"Not a problem." The thought raced through her mind, *After all, how hard can it be to make a banana cream pie, especially if it is legal to ask for help.*

"Okay, then. On Saturday at one o'clock, I'll meet you at your house for a slice of pie."

"Okay. Banana cream pie," said Katee.

"Right. Then we can go out for dinner."

"Okay. To a nice place and I'm buying."

"Okay. I'm picking the place. After that, we can go to a movie and I'm paying for the movie."

"Okay. Sounds good." Katee closed her book and stuffed it back into her book bag.

"And no telling anyone. I don't want Chaz sticking his nose in."

"Okay. I won't tell anyone. This will be our date." Katee's tone was firm. Now she wanted to get out the door before Ty changed his mind. Not that he would change his mind, but Katee did not want Chaz to enter into the conversation. She zipped her bag closed, slinging it over her shoulder as she stood and headed for the door. "Saturday…my house…one o'clock for banana cream pie. I…will…be…there." There was a certain sound to her voice that left no doubt as to her intentions. She would not be the cause of erroneous connections this time.

"Just don't expect a corsage. I gave that to Mom."

"That's fine. I don't need one."

"Okay," Ty said a little more softly, following Katee to the door. He watched as she bounded off the front step.

She hurried to her car. The driver's door was on the far side, away from the house. Katee tossed her bag into the car. She had just started to get into the car when Ty called to her.

"Hey. I thought you wanted help with your math."

Katee called back, "I'll get it later." Her head popped up over the roof of the car. "I've got to go learn how to make a pie, banana cream." She smiled broadly. "See ya."

She climbed into the car. As she drove away, she waved to Ty.

Minutes later, Katee pulled into the Robertses' drive.

Keri and Trace had migrated to the living room. Hearing the sound of a car, it was Keri who was first to take note. "Must be Katee."

Trace held up crossed fingers.

"I'll second that," Keri said. "I am so tired of the moping."

Katee almost danced through the front door. She glanced at the two girls and headed into the kitchen area. "You get your accounting all done?"

The mere fact that she asked such a question put Keri on alert. "Oh, yeah. Not a problem." Without saying it aloud, she mouthed to Trace, "She wants us to ask."

Trace nodded with a wink of an eye. "So how did it go with my brother? Was he civil?"

"It ...went...great." Katee belabored each word for emphasis as she laid her book bag on the dining table, adding, "But I can't tell you the details. That's part of the deal."

"You can't tell your own sister? Whose idea was that?" Keri asked.

"Ty's." Katee fought back a grin. "You know where Mom keeps her recipe book?"

Katee knew full well where her mother's recipe book was stored. There was some pleasure in toying with her older sister.

"Same place as always. Why do you need that? Planning on making something?"

"Just need a paper weight," said Katee.

"You should use your dictionary. You never use it anyway," said Keri.

The two made "gotcha faces" at one another.

Trace chuckled at the exchange. "So what do you want to make?"

"A pie...a banana cream pie."

"I see," Trace said, finding a slight corner of the secret unveiled. "You're lucky he didn't say gooseberry; that's really his favorite. Be hard to find gooseberries this time of year."

"He likes gooseberry pie?" Katee asked. A slight blush was taking over her face. She really wanted to tell the whole story, but Ty hadn't said there could be any exceptions to the "no tell" part of their arrangement.

"Yep, the more sour the better. He has a weird sense of taste."

Katee laughed at the comment. "I don't suppose either of you know how to make a banana cream pie."

"You mean you would let me help?" Keri asked in disbelief.

"Yes. I would let you help, providing you know how to make the pie. So...do you know how to make a banana cream pie?" Katee was encouraged by the prospect of having a knowledgeable assistant in the pie-making venture.

"Well...actually," Keri looked to Trace, who was shaking her head indicating she would be of no help, "I'm not really a pie maker."

Katee narrowed her eyes and clenched her lips giving her sister the "don't mess with me" look.

Keri swallowed, then had an idea. "Hey, why don't you call Grandma? She makes great pies."

Katee snapped her fingers and pointed to Keri. "Great idea. I think we'll keep you around."

"Gee, thanks."

Katee retrieved her phone and made the call.

"Hi, Grandma. How are you?"

After exchanging some pleasantries Katee said, "Here's the main reason I'm calling, do you know how to make a banana cream pie? Fantastic! Would I be able to come over Friday evening and have you help me make a pie?"

"Hey, make two pies. Trace and I should get one too," Keri said.

Katee waved at her to not interrupt. After finishing making the arrangements with her grandmother, she ended the call. "Okay, that takes care of that. I'm set."

"So let's see now," Keri said, turning to Trace. "She needs to make a pie."

"Pies, remember she is making two, one for me and you," Trace cut in.

"That's right, two pies on Friday night. So she must need them for Saturday. I am guessing there is to be a little get together at that time."

"Shut...up," Katee tried to keep from smiling and blushing, but her efforts were futile. "You don't know anything, and I didn't tell you anything. Got it."

"We got it," Trace said, giving her patented wink. "I'll keep Keri in line too. So don't worry."

"What do you mean...keep me in line?" Keri was incredulous.

The weekend would end soon enough. Katee went to her grandmother's house to make a list of ingredients that would be needed for the pies. She wanted to make certain everything was ready. She made arrangements to be sure Saturday would not be her day to work. Her dress went to the cleaners. It would be back on Thursday, without fail, she insisted on knowing. Only after she felt that every *t* was crossed and every *i* was dotted did she allow herself to dream of the perfect afternoon and evening.

It was apparent that something had changed at both the Roberts and Henry households; a cloud had been lifted. Keri and Trace tried their best to not let on that they knew anything, although both were questioned by their parents—mothers in particular.

"Don't knock it," Keri had told her mother. "Sure beats her being crabby about everything."

Ty's mom, Mary, asked Trace, "Ty seems more upbeat, don't you think?"

"Oh, I don't know. He has such mood swings. It's a guy thing, you know. I wouldn't get too excited about it. He'll probably be grumpy tomorrow."

At school, Katee didn't know what to expect. Would Ty talk to her or should they both pretend nothing was up? If he wants to keep this a secret, they would have to be "cool" toward one another. *What about after Saturday? Saturday would be great*, so thought Katee, *then it would not be a secret anymore*. Okay, she would try not to let on that anything had changed since last Friday unless Ty said something. This could be difficult.

Ty did not say anything.

He did, however, steal an occasional look, chastising himself for it after the fact. He half expected this latest plan would somehow crash and burn just as it had a little over a week earlier. Maybe it was ridiculous to hope for anything better. Ty was anything but comfortable around girls. His confidence level was lacking to say the least. His previous attempt at befriending a girl had not ended so well. To add to his insecurity, this was Katee. Surely, every other guy on the planet saw the same things he did. She was attractive, intelligent, and easy to talk to. She was…she was Katee. How could she possibly like Ty and not be interested in anyone else? So Ty reasoned, anyway. If he could just make it through Saturday, then if they never went out again, he would at least have that.

Thus, their week would go, occasionally glancing each others' direction, but only when they thought the other was not looking. They tried not to be obvious and gave the appearance of disinterest.

They were doing a good job of ignoring each other this way until Thursday of that week.

The economics class had gone to the library to do some research. Teej and Katee were sitting across from each other at a table, along with two other students. Ty and three others were sitting at the table adjacent to theirs, across the aisle and facing Katee. Suddenly, without warning, one of those moments—for no particular reason—occurred. They both decided to steal a glance at the same instant. The glance turned into a slightly prolonged look. Embarrassed, both turned away; they had to get back to work. It would not have presented a problem had it not been for the ever-attentive Teej, who noticed right away.

"Ah-hum," Teej cleared her throat.

Katee made eye contact, gave her best "I didn't do anything" look and returned her focus to her book.

"Hey," Teej whispered. "What was that?"

"Shush," replied Katee.

Teej was undeterred. "Are you and Ty—Ouch!" Her question was abruptly interrupted. It started as a whisper, but the "Ouch" came out loud and clear. She clapped her hand over her mouth and drew the stares of everyone in the surrounding area.

Giving a more stern look to her friend, Katee turned to a blank page of her notebook and wrote: *"Don't say another word and that means not to anyone. I'll fill you in later!"*

Teej mouthed the word "Okay." Then she reached down and rubbed her lower leg where Katee had kicked her. A little miffed, she grabbed Katee's notebook and wrote: *"Geez that really hurt!"*

Katee mouthed back, "Sorry," along with an expression that conveyed she really meant it.

The subject was never broached again that day, at least not until the two were belted into Teej's car. It was her turn to drive.

"Okay, so let's have it," Teej said before starting the car.

"Have what?" Katee asked.

"You know what. You said you would tell me later. Well, it's later, so what's going on with you and Ty?"

"Oh, that. It's not enough later. I can't tell you yet. But I will… later."

This double talk was met with a frown from Teej.

"I'll tell you when I can. I just can't tell you yet," Katee tried to explain in an apologetic manner.

"And when will this be?"

"Sunday," Katee said thoughtfully. She had that "don't be mad at me" look, an expression of innocence. In fact, she had that particular expression mastered.

"Sunday…so that means you two must be doing something Saturday night."

"Teej! Stop it!" Katee growled. "I said I would tell you everything on Sunday. Now drop it. And don't you dare say anything to anyone, not Denny or anyone, or I won't be your friend anymore."

"Calm down already. I won't say any more about it. I don't see why you want to keep it such a secret."

"I'm not the one who wants to keep it a secret," Katee said, relaxing a bit as she nibbled at a hangnail.

"So then, it's Ty… Oh, I get it. He doesn't want something happening like what happened at homecoming. I guess I can't blame him." Teej could see Katee peeking at her out of the corner of her eye, slightly nodding her head yes. "I knew something was up. You've been acting more normal this week. You'd better call me on Sunday, and I want details."

"I will," Katee said, a huge smile filling her face. "You know I will."

Friday night's football game did not go the way that Hillcrest fans and players had hoped it would. There were many who were quick to explain what had happened. It had been a good season, albeit no playoffs. The volleyball girls had a good season as well, although they would lose in the district final.

The season-ending losses were of little concern at the Robertses' house. The chaos there on Saturday morning was of a more pressing nature. Pies had been successfully made the night before. Katee hurried to her grandmother's house to retrieve them. They were then dutifully placed in a cleared out spot in the refrigerator with a note: *Do Not Touch the Pie or Die.*

It was shortly after 11 a.m., and the preparation ritual had just begun. Deanne Roberts was in the kitchen thinking about what might be good for lunch. Keri was just returning from a quick trip to the grocery store. Thad Roberts had gone to the golf course, trying to squeeze in a final round of play before weather made it impossible to do so.

As Keri was putting the grocery items away, she noticed the note attached to the pies. The fridge door still open, she called in a loud voice, "Hey, these pies look awfully good. Wonder if anyone would notice if I use a finger and have a little taste?"

"You are going to get in trouble," her mother warned.

Sure enough, moments later, Katee appeared at the top of the stairway. "You touch the pie and you die."

Keri cackled with delight. "You're so much fun."

"Yeah, well I'm not kidding around. Mom, watch her," Katee said with a serious look.

Keri returned the look then clapped her hands in delight.

Katee shook her head and returned to her preparation, inwardly laughing, knowing she had just made her sister's morning by playing along.

Grilled cheese sandwiches won out for the midday meal. Mrs. Roberts called the girls to lunch.

Katee bounded down the stairs. "Ty will be here at one o'clock. I need to finish getting ready."

"You have time for a glass of milk and a sandwich; you can have the pie for dessert when Ty comes."

"We have to wait till Ty gets here for dessert?" Keri said. "I don't know if I can wait that long. Those pies look really good. Are you sure Grandma didn't just make them?"

"Grandma told me what to do. I made the pies. And you can have your pie after Ty and I leave." Katee gave a toothless smile, before taking a bite of her sandwich. She would put her older sister in her place.

"Ahh," Keri grunted, feigning incredulity. She was glad to see Katee enjoying this so much.

But Katee's little slip caught Mom's attention. "Oh, so you two are going somewhere?"

Katee had only told her mother that she was making a banana cream pie and Ty was coming over.

"Yeah, we're planning on going out," Katee said hesitantly.

"I see. That's good to know. Remember, home by eleven thirty."

"Yep. I remember," Katee relaxed, taking a drink of milk. That is, she relaxed until she noticed the time. "Oh my gosh, I've got to finish getting ready," she said as she stood up and chugged the remainder of her milk before rushing to the stairs.

"I thought he's not coming until one," Keri said.

"I want to be ready by twelve forty-five."

"I think you should shoot for twelve thirty," Keri said.

"Stop that," Mom directed Keri.

"I'm just kidding. She can take it."

Mom and Keri cleared the table and readied it for Katee's guest. Keri good-naturedly chided her mother that Katee should be doing this.

"She'll do the same for you sometime," was her mom's response.

It was 12:45 on the nose when Katee emerged at the top of the stairs. "Okay, what do think?" She began her grand descent down the stairway.

"You look beautiful," was Mom's assessment.

"Ehh, you'll do." Keri tried to be less impressed, adding, "You might even look better than you did homecoming night."

"Thanks." Katee blushed. "I hope so." She really wanted to make things right. There was still the sense of guilt, not so much for what had happened, the date that never happened, but rather that Ty had missed out on the homecoming event. It was a special night. That Chaz had been a jerk and messed up the evening, that was a given. But…homecoming was a special night that could not be replaced. There was not a do-over. For that reason, Katee felt like she owed it to Ty to make this a memorable first date. It wouldn't be homecoming, but it could still be a special time.

Keri had her instructions, disappear until Ty and Katee had left. Her reward, then she could have some pie. "Gee, thanks," Keri had told her sister.

The remaining minutes seemed to drag toward one o'clock. It was 12:55 when the doorbell rang. Keri piped up, "You want me to get that?"

For the briefest of moments, Katee thought about saying yes. After all, "what if" by some cruel fluke of fate it was Chaz. She would have died on the spot or at the very least flown off the handle in a fit of unbridled rage. No…this could not be Chaz. Surely, he had no way of knowing. It had to be Ty.

"No, I'll get it," Katee replied. She straightened her dress, took a last quick look in the mirror, everything seemed to be in place. Hand on the door knob, one last deep breath, exhale. *Here we go.* She opened the door. There stood Ty. "Hi, right on time," she greeted him with a smile.

Ty took a moment to gain his composure, finally saying with a hint of nervousness, "Ah, hi, you look…breathtaking."

"Thanks," said Katee, glowing in the compliment. "You look great too. I like the jacket. Come on in. The pie is ready. I hope you'll like it."

"Oh, almost forgot. This is for you. It's not a corsage, but Mom said I should bring something, so I thought candy."

"Good choice. Tell your mom thanks too." Katee could not keep from smiling.

"I'll be sure to. I got a large box. Trace said I needed to bring some extra candy since Keri would probably want some."

"What's that?" called a voice from in the den, just off the living room. Keri peeked out of the room. "Did I here my name mentioned in the same sentence as candy?"

Deanne tugged on Keri's shirt trying to pull her back out of sight, all to no avail. "Get back in here."

"But they have candy, and I get to have some."

Katee shook her head, smiling all the while, "I was going to lock her in the bathroom, but Mom vetoed that idea…You guys just as well come on out and have some pie with us."

Ty nodded his approval.

"Now that's more like it." Keri pulled away from her mother's tug. "Come on, Mom. You get to meet Ty." Keri walked straight to Ty. "Hello, Ty," she said, throwing her arms around him, giving him a hug.

Ty didn't know what to think. He managed to say, "Hi," while looking to Katee for guidance. She just shrugged.

Releasing Ty from her grasp, Keri straightened his jacket for him, looked toward Katee and said with a wink, "Nice."

Katee held her hand to her face to hide a smile and prevent an all-out laughing attack. Composing herself, she managed an introduction, "Mom, this is Ty."

Keri stepped back and Mrs. Roberts extended her hand. "Hello, Ty. You must feel like you just walked into a sitcom."

Ty chuckled, accepting her hand, "Oh, it's okay. I have a sister, too, you know. She happens to be friends with Keri. That tells a lot."

"Uh, I may have to tell Trace you said that." Keri wheeled to go to the kitchen. "I'll serve the pie." She walked past Katee. "You should have said 'Entrée' when you asked him in. It would have sounded more refined. You know what I mean?"

"Uh huh," Katee said.

All seated themselves at the table, while Keri served. "Anyone need anything to drink?" Keri asked. "We have tea, lemonade, milk, and water."

Katee exchanged a glance with Ty then placed her order, as did the others.

Sampling the pie, Ty could break the ice. "This is good."

"Thank you," Katee said.

"Grandma told her how to make it," Keri felt the need to add.

Katee's eyes widened, glaring at her sister.

"We don't want any false pretenses," Keri said in response to Katee's facial expression while forking herself a bite of pie.

"It was legal for me to have help." Katee looked to Ty for confirmation and received it.

"Yes it was," Ty said. "And this is really good pie."

All agreed, and there was some discussion about Katee's grandmother's pie-making expertise. Katee said she may want to try her hand at further pie-baking since it was so much fun this time.

During a lull in the conversation, Keri asked, "So, may I ask where you two are going?"

Katee turned to Ty awaiting a response.

"Well, I was hoping to keep that secret from Katee until we were on the road for a while." Seeing the deflated reaction of both Katee and Keri, Ty quickly added, "Your mom knows where we are going. She can tell you after we're gone."

"How do you get to know?" Both girls turned to their mother. It was Keri who asked the question.

"Well, if you must know," she said, "Ty spoke to me earlier this week and asked permission to take Katee out to dinner and a movie."

"You knew all along." Katee said. "I thought I was going to get into trouble."

Mom shrugged. "Nope, you are not getting into trouble. It was very thoughtful of Ty to ask permission to take you to this restaurant. And I already told Ty, don't worry about the curfew. We don't want you rushing to get home."

"That means you're going out of town," Keri deduced. "You dog."

Katee returned a smile. "Guess so."

"We ought to get going. The movie will start at seven. We want to allow enough time for dinner." Ty had it all planned. "You have Mom's cell phone number, right?" he asked Mrs. Roberts.

She nodded to the affirmative.

"She has my number too," Katee said.

"Yes, I do, smarty. However, I will only call if there is an emergency. You, I expect to hear from, when you get to the restaurant, are at the movie, and again when you are in the car heading home."

"Yes, ma'am." Katee gave a playful salute.

"Not to worry Mrs. Roberts, we will be sure to check in. I have orders to call my mom, too," Ty said with a smile. Ty turned to Katee, "I just hope you are not going to be on your phone all evening."

"Uh, I am not going to be on my phone all evening. In fact, I'll put it on silent and will only look at it when we get to where we are eating, after dinner, and after the movie. They'll have to be turned off at the movie. And…and I won't call anyone except for mom…unless there's an emergency."

"Yeah, right. You'll explode," Keri said.

"Not funny, Keri. And you stay out of this," Katee said.

"Maybe it was a little funny," Ty said. "We won't worry about the phone for now. We should get going."

What followed was the barrage of send offs that usually accompany such events. Katee threw in a "don't wait up for me" for Keri's benefit. Katee kissed her mother's cheek and whispered, "Thank you."

Deanne nodded and returned the kiss. "You have a good time."

Ty and Katee were out the door when Keri said in a loud voice that even they could hear, "So where are they going?"

"Oh, you! Wait till they are out of the drive and I'll tell you."

Katee laughed. "That's my sis."

"I know. Big sisters, aren't they great?"

Minutes later they were on the road, the highway that would take them to the interstate. Katee could contain herself no longer. "So, are we going to Mister Q's?"

"No. I still don't even know where that is."

"I can show you. We're going that direction." As they neared the interstate interchange, "Just go straight here."

Ty followed Katee's directions.

"There it is on the left." Katee pointed to the huge sign that was the land mark for the restaurant, Mister Q's.

Ty turned into the parking lot to survey the area. "Hmmm. Guess if I would have just gone straight I would have found it."

A little uncomfortable, Katee nibbled at a hangnail, which she may or may not have actually had. "Yeah," she said quietly, a touch of nervousness in her voice. She really didn't want to relive homecoming night.

"You know, I've been thinking. I should have asked your neighbor how to get here. She probably could have told me."

"Yeah, that's right," Katee perked up.

"Might have been an awful scene when I showed up."

"It would have been better than what happened." Her tone had become serious, almost sullen in a way as she recalled the gamut of emotions she had endured the past couple of weeks. This whole discussion was putting a damper on the evening as far as Katee was concerned.

"Maybe I should have helped make the pie, huh?"

"Maybe you should have," Katee smiled, almost laughing.

"I suppose I could help next time."

"Sure, we could make a gooseberry pie. I don't think we would have to make two. Keri wouldn't like one." Katee watched to see the reaction from Ty.

"You know how to make gooseberry pie?" Ty asked excitedly, much to the delight of Katee. "Wait a minute. How did you know?"

"Ha, ha. Trace told me, another big sister moment."

"It figures," Ty said. "Oh well. It's not here that we are dining." He pointed the car toward the exit so they could return to the interstate exchange.

"So where are we going? You know, I'm probably the only one who doesn't know. I am betting even Keri has pried it out of Mom by now."

"Likely so. Have you ever heard of Sherman House?"

"Sherman House! Good choice. We went with Mom and Dad there a couple years ago. It's a nice place. A bit of a drive though. No wonder Mom said we could be a little late getting back. You know, you probably scored some big time points asking her first."

"Oh, I just thought it was the thing to do. I promised we would not be in a hurry, and we'd check in after dinner, and then again before we head home. There is a nice movie theater right by the restaurant, so it will be convenient."

The evening went well. The conversation was good, comfortable for both. It was the bus ride and the Saturday at Ty's place when Katee first asked about going to homecoming all over. Dutifully, Katee messaged her mom upon arrival and again after dinner; Ty checked in with his mother as well. Dinner was great! Katee paid for the meal, while Ty covered the tip. Katee got to pick the movie. The film was a comedy; Ty paid. They both gave it a lukewarm rating. A phone call to both Moms was followed by a pleasant ride home.

Ty walked Katee to the door.

"I really enjoyed this evening," Ty said, a little unsure of how to end an evening that had gone so well.

"Me too." Katee paused then quickly added, "Maybe we can do something next week."

"Yeah, I'd like that."

"It doesn't have to cost a lot either," Katee said. She didn't want Ty thinking they had to go to a full dinner restaurant every time. It was the companionship she was interested in.

"All the better," Ty said. "I guess I should let you go. Your sis is probably waiting up for you."

"Probably," Katee said with a laugh.

"I'll see you Monday, if not before." He turned, walking down the drive. Looking over his shoulder, he waved back to Katee.

She smiled and returned the wave. "See ya."

Katee went on in, and sure enough, there was Keri on the couch. Mom and Dad had already turned in, although they were likely still awake.

"Well?" Keri asked.

"A plus," said Katee. Both girls squealed with delight.

"Everything, I've got to know, and don't leave anything out."

"All right, all right, but I've got to call Teej. I'll put it on speaker."

"You think she's still up?"

"Oh, I know she's still up. Probably has the phone in her hand."

"Hello," Teej answered.

"I just got home. Ty and I went to Sherman House and then a movie," Katee shared excitedly.

"You went to Sherman House! No way!"

The rest was girl talk, Katee telling the story, while Keri and Teej listened, interjecting frequently.

Ty pulled into the drive. He had been thinking about the evening and Katee as he drove the short distance home. After getting out of the car, he paused, propping himself against the car, slipping his thumbs into the pockets of his slacks. He listened to the quiet of the night, a car not too far off and the screech of some unseen animal. The sky was black and full of stars. There was no moon to be seen.

Ty stared at the stars for several minutes before whispering, "Dad, I really like her…But how will I know?" He didn't say anything else. Keeping the remainder of his question to himself, unsure what to ask or maybe embarrassed to ask it of his father.

Regardless, one of those annoying tears had found its way to the corner of his eye. He dried it with the swipe of his hand, then righted himself. Most likely Trace and Mom would be waiting, eager for the report that Ty would gladly share.

Ty would have to wait for an answer from the stars. He and Katee would share more time in the coming weeks as they learned more about one another. Their dates were not as formal as the trip to Sherman House, to be sure, but the signs were all good that this might be a lasting relationship. That is, until one cold night in December.

Chapter Eight

The fall of the year had been a good one. The leaves had turned; vibrant gold and red gave color to wooded areas. The change from fall to winter activities made its transition as well. Football and volleyball gave way to basketball and wrestling. The season ending disappointments were soon forgotten; the accomplishments now seemed more rewarding.

Ty and Katee spent more time together. It seemed so natural. No, their times together were not as formal as their trip to Sherman House, rather, it was sharing an ice cream or taking a walk or going to a movie or doing homework together.

There was also the play and Katee's big performance. Ty was in the back row, impressed by Katee's talent; he was one of her biggest fans. Ty knew that others must surely be as enamored with Katee as he was. But the closer they became, the less confident he was with what she saw in him. *She can have any guy she wants*, he thought. *And there are a lot of guys who want to be with her.* The insecurity Ty felt was of his own making. From Katee's point of view, she had struck gold. She had found a guy who made her feel the way a girl should feel and she wasn't interested in anybody else.

Coaches, players, and fans encouraged Ty to go out for the winter sports. He had other ideas, though. He didn't see himself as talented in either basketball or wrestling; instead, he wanted to concentrate on preparing for the upcoming track season. He had looked up the times from last year's state track meet, and felt with a little improvement he could compete for a state title. The school had a well-stocked weight room, complete with treadmill, stationary bikes, and a wide array of weight equipment.

Katee was very supportive. In fact, she offered to train with him when time allowed, winking as she said so. For now, her priority was to begin preparation for the speech contests in February. Plus, there would be a spring play. She hoped to talk Ty into trying out for the spring play. Ty was noncommittal, but it was still early, and he hadn't said no.

The winter winds had arrived and along with them, the first snows. There were probably four to five inches of snow on the ground. School had let out for winter break. Christmas celebrations had come and gone. The New Year would begin in a few days.

Ty and Katee planned an evening at the bowling alley along with Denny and Teej. The bowling alley had a game room and concession area as well. For thirty dollars, a couple kids could have a fun evening complete with something to eat and drink. Ty and Katee would meet Teej and Denny at the bowling alley. They would need to take Katee's car. Ty's pickup was having heater issues; it was in the garage for repairs. Katee didn't mind. She preferred her car to the pickup.

They had played some pool and pinball; had a sandwich, fries, and a soda; and just finished a third game of bowling. Ty was returning the balls to the racks, Katee and Teej were returning the bowling shoes, and Denny was taking a call on his cell phone.

"Teej," Denny motioned to his now admitted girlfriend.

Teej joined Denny, while Katee and Ty rejoined one another, curious as to what the phone call was about. This is one mystery that would soon be revealed.

"That was Chaz," Teej sounded a little annoyed that he had called. "He wants to know if we could stop over to see his new… gigantic…big screen TV. It is really super fantastic," she said sarcastically, yawning for effect.

Denny tugged at her elbow. "Don't be that way."

"Can you guys come, too?" Teej asked, directing her question to both, but mostly toward Katee, hoping she would have the say.

Katee looked toward Ty. She knew he would not want to go. The expression on his face confirmed it.

"I don't want to be the only girl there," Teej implored, then added, "and Denny seems to think we need to go."

"Uh, don't put it all on me," Denny said. "We don't have to stay long. Just long enough to be impressed, then we can all leave."

Chaz had never quite reestablished himself with the Gang, although he had tried. For now, they were all on speaking terms; all except for Ty, but then he never spoke a lot to Chaz anyway. The issue was more a matter of trust. Denny was the most forgiving. Teej never really liked Chaz all that much. She reserved the right to think ill of him. Katee had squared things with Ty so she was no longer as mad at Chaz as she once was. In fact, she thought of him as a friend who occasionally did stupid things. Ty, on the other hand, wanted nothing to do with him, and since he was never part of the Gang anyway, what did it matter? He thought, *Chaz frequently did stupid things.*

"We won't have to stay long," Katee echoed. A long pause followed, then "Please?"

"Okay," Ty finally said with a sigh. "You know, I deserve a hug for this."

"Not a problem," Denny said, throwing his arms around Ty.

"Not what I had in mind," said Ty, watching the girls struggle to hold back the laughter.

"Here, I'll make it better," Teej said. As Denny released his hug, she took his place, wrapping her arms around Ty's neck and squeezing. "I really appreciate you doing this." She patted him on the shoulder.

"Me too," Katee took Teej's place hugging Ty. "I'm not getting left out of this hug-fest."

The drive to Chaz's would be a short one, but it was long enough for Ty to have the notion: *She could drop me off and go to Chaz's with Teej and Denny... But then, I guess that wouldn't be the right thing to do.*

Katee knew Ty was uncomfortable with going to Chaz's place. She could feel it.

"It'll be okay," she said lightheartedly, hoping to dispel some of his apprehension. It didn't seem to work. "He's really not a bad guy when you get to know him."

Ty turned his head toward Katee but didn't say a word. He may have grimaced a little. Hoping that went unnoticed, he turned his stare to the passenger's side window. He didn't say it, but he thought it, *Katee, you've got to be kidding. The guy is a full-of-himself moron.* It would not have served any useful purpose to have a discussion on the merits of Chaz Thomas's character, at least not now. So, Ty refrained from commenting, much to Katee's disappointment.

She had hoped to somehow be a peacemaker, allowing Ty to forgive Chaz. Perhaps the two could even be friends and Ty would feel more at home with the Gang. Katee wanted to be friends with everyone. She did just want one…special…boyfriend, but that shouldn't preclude her from having lots of other friends. This did not mean that she liked everyone she ever met. Somehow though, she did not see any contradiction in her feelings.

They pulled into the Thomases' drive. Katee parked behind Denny's car. The four walked to the house together.

After the doorbell rang, Chaz appeared. "Hey, guys. Come on in. Let me take your coats." They all obliged, except for Ty. He was wearing a letter jacket from his old school. He felt more comfortable with it on; plus, he intended for this to be a short visit.

There were others there: Tammy, Lisa, Cathy, Dave, and Luke, all of whom were from out of town. Chaz made the introductions, introducing Tammy as his girlfriend and Katee as his old girlfriend, with a laugh.

"Hi," Katee extended her hand to Tammy. "He is talking about way ancient when referring to me. We are just friends."

"Oh, admit it, you still have a flame for me," said Chaz.

Chaz ignored the glaring look that Katee gave in return. If he hoped for a reaction from Ty, he was disappointed.

"Hey, wait till you guys see the set. It makes you feel like you're in the game," said Chaz as he led the way to entertainment room, complete with big screen TV, pool table, card table, and seating area. There was also a kitchenette with microwave and small refrigerator. It was a nice set up. Chaz was more than eager to show it off.

Denny gave Ty a knowing look.

Ty shook his head slightly, then took a deep breath, thinking, *Gee there are other girls here, so Teej shouldn't need Katee. We should be able to go ahead and leave.*

Katee fawned over the room a bit, how nice it was, such a great place to watch a movie, as good as going to a theater. Chaz ate it up. The others were in the room, and they were talking, but Chaz was focused on Katee, flattered by what he perceived as the attention she was giving him.

Tammy was a little annoyed, but she knew Chaz's ways. The thought of dumping him had occurred to her and was nearing a reality.

Ty was a little annoyed, but he knew Katee was just trying to be nice.

Chaz explained that his parents would be out of town for the rest of the week, so this would be "party central," in his words. He played the party host, offering everyone drinks. He had soda and beer. He mentioned the beer in hopes of ramping up the party idea. The new arrivals all declined. Chaz knew none of the Gang drank alcohol, and he figured Ty to be of that mold as well. He had plenty of snacks. Katee could not resist sampling some chips and dip.

They had been there for over a half an hour. Ty was getting a little restless. He was standing by the doorway to the entertainment room. That was his subtle way of suggesting to Katee it was time to go. She didn't seem to take the hint, at least not right away. The girls were having a chatter-fest; Chaz and the other guys, minus Ty, tried to bull their way into the conversation.

Finally, Katee noticed Ty by the doorway. She glanced at her watch. "Gosh, looks like it is about time to get going. It was really nice meeting all of you."

"We should go, too," Teej said to Denny.

"You guys and your curfews; I feel for you," Chaz said.

"It's not that bad," said Katee, sounding almost gleeful. "Keeps us out of trouble."

The group all moved toward the front of the house where they had entered. As they did so, Chaz whispered something to Dave and Luke. The three laughed and seemed to agree on whatever the private joke was.

The entry area of the house was almost like the lobby of a hotel. There was some seating, a coat closet where guests put their coats, and an ornamental basket for umbrellas that also held a couple of canes for show. There was a stairway that led to the second story, at the top of which was a landing with benches and a flower arrangement.

"Hey Katee, come here, I've got something I want to show you," Chaz said in his usual "do as I say" tone. He was near the top of the stairs before looking back to see if she was following. "Come on, it'll just take a second."

"Okay already," Katee answered. "I'll be there in a second."

Excusing herself from the others, she followed Chaz up the stairs, not wondering for even a moment what Chaz might have on his mind to show her and much too obediently for Ty's liking. She didn't notice that Luke and Dave had positioned themselves at the bottom of the stairway.

Teej and Denny had located their coats. Expecting Katee to join them in a few minutes, Teej retrieved Katee's coat for her as well.

Ty watched as Katee met Chaz at the top of the stairway.

"Come in here."

Katee took two steps toward the room and realized "in here" was Chaz's bedroom. That realization ignited her better judgment. "Wait. I'm not going in there alone."

"Oh come on," Chaz grabbed Katee by the arm.

"No, Chaz," shouted Katee, offering some resistance. It was all for naught; Chaz stepped behind her, lifted and carried her into the bedroom, despite her efforts to prevent him from doing so.

He tossed her effortlessly onto the bed and closed and locked the door behind them. "Shush. It's just a joke."

Katee rolled off the far side of the bed away from Chaz. "I'm not seeing anything funny."

"Just play along. It'll make Tammy jealous." He took off his shirt in a quick motion.

"Put that back on," Katee shouted. "Chaz, I'll start screaming." The volume of her voice increased loud enough to be heard by the others in the house.

"It's just a joke." Then he started making noises, most would call obscene, obnoxious things that would certainly embarrass his parents.

"Chaz," Katee tried not to laugh. "You are so stupid." She could not help turning a little red-faced.

Proud of himself, Chaz chuckled, "That should get them excited." He unbuckled his belt and messed his hair as he reached to open the door.

Ty was watching as Chaz grabbed Katee, dragging her into the room at the top of the stairs. He didn't hesitate. He bolted toward the stairway only to find the smirking Luke and Dave guarding the way.

"Easy big guy, they are just going to have a little fun." Luke held up both arms in front of his body to block Ty.

Ty wasn't of the mind to discuss the matter. With a sweeping motion of his left arm, he knocked Luke's arms from in front of him. At nearly the same instant, with his right hand, he caught Luke just below the left shoulder on his chest.

The move took Luke by surprise, causing him to lose his balance and fall into Dave. The two tumbled to the floor, losing their smirks as they fell.

Ty raced up the steps, two at a time. He heard Katee shouting and Chaz grunting. Teej and Denny had reacted a beat slower than Ty, but they weren't far behind. Teej grabbed a cane from the umbrella basket, dropping Katee's coat as she rushed to help her friend. Now she stood on the first step of the stairway, the cane raised menacingly above her head, Denny at her side.

"Stay put." Teej ordered Luke and Dave.

"Better do as she says," Denny said. He was not going to leave Teej to keep the two back by herself. It would be up to Ty to rescue Katee.

"Okay, okay. Relax already. We were just joking around."

The other three girls, Tammy and friends, were in shock. Neither Cathy nor Lisa knew what to say. Tammy was boiling. Finally, Tammy said, "Let's get out of here." Her anger level was growing. She was not a happy person at the moment. Finding their coats, the three headed for the door. Tammy snarled, "I hope they beat some sense into all of them." There did not seem to be much disagreement from the other two girls.

When Ty reached the top of the stairs, he tried the knob. The door seemed to be locked. It did not occur to Ty to knock, the situation being what it was. Instead, his next move was to plant his right foot squarely against the door, centimeters to the right of the knob, with a shattering blow, the likes of which showed no mercy. The door would be ruined, as would the door frame and the hardware for the door knob.

As the door burst open, it smacked Chaz in his left hand as he reached for the knob on the opposite side. "What the…" Surprised by the door that seemed to explode in front of him, Chaz took a step backward.

Ty followed the door into the room. He saw Chaz, bare-chested, belt unfastened, and had heard Katee shout moments before. That was all the reason he needed, his right fist caught Chaz squarely on the left jaw.

Chaz fell like a tree in the forest. He didn't know what hurt worse, his jaw or his hand. The expletives poured out of his mouth as he lay on the floor, feeling his jaw with his right hand while holding his left gingerly to his body.

Katee gasped. "Ty…it was just a joke." Wide-eyed, she tried to comprehend what had just happened. She had never seen Ty in fighting mode nor did she want him to continue. Chaz looked as though he had been conquered. How could she diffuse the situation?

"He was just joking. He wasn't harming anything."

She saw the trickle of blood at Chaz's mouth. "Oh God, you're bleeding." A box of tissue was on the night stand. Katee rushed to Chaz's side, box in hand.

"We need some ice," Katee said to Ty, still flustered by the recent events.

Ty was bewildered. He rushed in to save Katee, the hero looking to slay the villain and rescue the damsel in distress. Now it would seem the damsel was sympathetic toward the villain. Never mind that Ty may have hurt his own foot or hand, kicking down the door and giving the hard-headed Chaz the fist to the chops that he had long had coming. Never mind that Chaz had dragged Katee into the bedroom despite her protests. Nope, now she wanted him to go get ice. A stupefying turn of events. A little dazed, Ty walked out of the room and slowly down the steps.

"Is Katee okay?" Teej asked in a panic.

"Yeah, I guess so," Ty answered, still seemingly in a fog. "She wants some ice," he added, "for Chaz."

Teej and Denny exchanged glances.

"I'll get the ice. You check on Katee," Denny said.

"Okay," Teej nodded and raced up the stairs.

The cane still clutched in her hand, she looked at Ty quizzically as she passed. He shook his head in disbelief.

Ty made it to the bottom of the stairs where Luke and Dave still loitered. They exchanged glares but no one spoke, at least not until Ty had left the room, actually, left the house. Only then did Luke grunt something about a sucker punch; he'd like to see him try that again.

Teej found Katee kneeling beside Chaz. She overheard Katee telling Chaz that everything would be okay, that Ty would pay for the damage to the door.

Just then Katee noticed Teej in the room. "Is someone getting the ice?"

"Yeah, sure, Denny is," said Teej. Then she thought, *Are you sure you don't want to borrow this cane and whack him a few times first? He really doesn't look that hurt to me.*

Katee stood up, turned her back to Chaz and whispered to Teej, "Ty hit him."

"Only once?" asked Teej.

Katee made a face and nodded. "Chaz wants to call the police and sue Ty for damages. We need to calm him down."

"I doubt if he's hurt as badly as he is letting on and it's his own fault. We'll take care of him. You had better go check on Ty."

"Oh," Katee said, as if startled into the realization that Ty was no longer in the room and might need some comforting. "Okay, I'll talk to you later."

Katee exited the room, meeting Denny on the stairs.

"Got the ice," Denny said, holding up a plastic bag.

"Did you see where Ty went?"

Denny shrugged. "I haven't seen him since I went for this."

"He went outside," Dave said, overhearing the question from the bottom of the stairs. "Must've been five minutes ago."

"Thanks."

Katee saw her coat lying on the floor where Teej had dropped it before all the commotion. Continuing down the stairs she retrieved the coat and pulled it on.

She went outside and called, "Ty!" Hearing no response, she called again more loudly, "Ty!" It felt as though it had gotten colder since they had left the bowling alley. There was definitely a chill in the air. Fortunately, there was little in the way of a breeze. *He must've started walking home*, she thought.

Her keys were in her coat, just where she had left them. She would take her car and catch up with Ty. There was only the one road directly to Ty's grandpa's place, down the pavement a mile and a half, then left at the corner a half a mile on the gravel road. Katee made the trip at a slow pace, keeping a watchful eye out for Ty. *He must be running*, she thought as she turned onto the gravel.

Moments later, she was at the Henrys' house. There was a light on in the kitchen. It was a little after eleven. Should she drive up and knock on the door? It was getting late and would take her at least ten minutes to get home before her curfew. She hadn't seen any sign of Ty on the road. He must've have made it home. She could talk to him in the morning. "I'll call Teej and let her know what's up. I wish Ty had a phone."

"Hello," Teej answered.

"I didn't find Ty. I'm guessing he went home. How's Chaz?"

"He's just spouting off right now, the way he usually does. He'll live, for now anyway. After his dad gets home, that may be a different matter."

"Well, I'm sure Ty will see the door gets fixed. Look, right now, I'm going on home. I'll go see Ty tomorrow, try to make things okay. I'll let you know how it goes."

"Okay, we're leaving here now, too. I think the crisis is over."

Teej hung up, then turned to Denny, who had just got into the driver's side of the car where Teej had been waiting. "I don't think Ty should have to pay for anything. Chaz got a taste of what he deserved."

"I know. I know. I don't think he will ever learn."

Katee was well within her curfew as she came in the front door of the Robertses' house.

Her dad was still up, giving the appearance of watching some old movie. Truth was, either he or his wife would always stay up, waiting for their children to arrive safely home. Now that Keri was older, they gave her more leeway although they still liked to know where she was at. This weekend Keri and Trace Henry had gone to Minnesota to spend some time at the home of a mutual college friend. She had checked in, so all was well. Katee was nearing that age when she would soon be leaving the nest and no longer under the curfew rule, just not quite yet. Thad and Deanne Roberts trusted their girls; that wasn't the point. It's always a parent's prerogative to worry; their rules were not unreasonable, so Katee was never surprised to find one or both of her parents waiting up for her.

"How was the bowling?" he asked.

"We had fun. I got a one sixty-five," Katee answered, blowing her father a kiss. "I'm going to bed."

Thad chuckled, then whispered, "That sounds like a good idea."

Minutes later he joined his wife in their bed. "She's home." Following a peck on the cheek and an affirming mumble from his wife, Thad would soon be fast asleep.

Katee made short work of readying herself for bed. Some final thoughts raced through her mind. *Chaz is such a pain. I hope Ty's not mad. Oh, it will all be better tomorrow. I just need to sleep.* She pulled the comforter around her shoulders. The warmth of her bed and the safety of home soon allowed her to relax and fall into a deep sleep.

The family was at rest. Still there were sounds, the ticking of a clock, the hum of the furnace, and even the occasional passing of a car outside. They were the noises of the night to which the Robertses were accustomed. It was the sound of the telephone ringing near their bedside that awoke the older Robertses.

The first ring startled both Thad and Deanne. Neither moved a muscle until the second ring. The phone was on Thad's side of the bed. With the second ring, he realized it was the phone and not the alarm. The clock showed 2:26 a.m. on the display. A chill of fright gripped both Thad and Deanne. Was this bad news? Why would anyone be calling at this time of night?

"Hello," Thad answered, sleepily.

"Hello, this is Mary Henry," the voice on the other end of the call responded with an obvious level of concern. "I am so sorry to bother you this time of night, but I was wondering, has Katee come home?"

"Well, yes," he said, surprised by the question while wiping the sleep from his eyes. "She got home about eleven." Thad motioned to his wife who was sitting upright, interested in the call. He covered the end of the receiver, "Go wake Katee."

Deanne felt the concern in her husband's voice and immediately swung herself out of bed, throwing on her robe as she quickly made the short walk to Katee's room. She found Katee sound asleep. Gently, she placed her hand on her daughter's shoulder. "Katee…honey…wake up." Her voice was soft, not wanting to startle Katee any more than need be.

Gradually, Katee left her dream world of deep sleep, waking to find her mother at her side. "Mom," she groaned. "What's going on?" The room was still dark, the only light coming from a night light in the hallway, making its way through the door that Deanne had left ajar.

Meanwhile, Thad had learned from Mary that Ty had not come home. Since he had gone out with Katee in Katee's car, she had expected Katee to bring him back home. All of this seemed very reasonable to Thad. His wife was waking Katee as they spoke. He would find out what Katee knew and call her right back.

"We need you to wake up," Deanne said, still with a reassuring air of calm that nothing was wrong.

Moments later, Thad entered the room with a greater sense of urgency than that of his wife, flicking the switch to the overhead light.

Katee reacted to the sudden burst of light. "Dad, geez!"

She covered her eyes in defense of the blinding light. It would take only a matter of seconds for her eyes to adjust.

"Did you take Ty home?"

"Uh, no," Katee answered, uncomfortable with the question.

She had picked him up; she should have taken him home. "Why not?"

"Dad. You're scaring her," said Deanne.

Thad turned to his wife with a look of slight impatience, "Ty never made it home. The Henrys are scared. I'm a little scared. We need to know what happened."

Turning back to his daughter, he said in no uncertain terms, "Now, you tell us what happened, don't leave anything out, and be very quick about it."

Katee's eyes were now wide open. "Okay…we went to the bowling alley: Teej, Denny, Ty, and me. When we finished, Chaz called and wanted us to stop by."

Thad's lips tightened. "Were his parents home?"

"No…anyway, Ty didn't want to go, but we talked him into it. There were some other kids there. Chaz showed us everything. We talked and ate some snacks. At about 10:30 or so, we started talking about leaving. Chaz said he had something upstairs he wanted to show me. I went to the top of the stairs. He wanted me to go into his room. It didn't feel right, so I told him I wouldn't go in alone. He grabbed me and carried me in. I yelled, but I couldn't stop him."

Thad was showing great restraint at this time. Deanne looked a little perplexed by the direction the story was taking.

"He closed the door and locked it. Then he took his shirt off and started making noises."

"What do you mean, making noises?" her mother asked.

"You know, like we were doing stuff," embarrassed, Katee said, "Like we were having sex or something."

Thad could refrain from comment no longer. "You've got to be kidding."

"He was just joking," Katee said in Chaz's defense. "He said he wanted to make Tammy, his new girlfriend, jealous."

"Okay, so what happened next?" Thad asked, his hands locked behind his neck, exasperated by the details, yet eager to move the story along.

"Well, Ty kicked the door in. Then…he hit Chaz in the mouth, knocking him to the floor."

Thad peeked at Deanne, who returned a glance of approval. "Way to go, Ty."

"Chaz was bleeding, so I got him some tissue. I thought Ty was going to get ice. Teej came in the room and said Denny was getting the ice and that I should check on Ty. The guys downstairs told me that Ty went outside. So I went out and called to him. He didn't answer, so I got in my car and drove to his place. I didn't see him anywhere on the road, so I figured he must have beaten me home. I called Teej, then came on home."

"What was Ty wearing?" her father asked.

"He had a letter jacket from his old school in Indiana, blue jeans, and sports shoes."

"Okay…Dee, you call Mrs. Henry; tell her what we know. The number is by the phone in the bedroom. I'll call the sheriff, then, retrace the route from the Henrys to the Thomases."

"What are you thinking?" asked Katee, the panic beginning to show in her voice.

"Something must have happened, or Ty would have gone home. It was to get into the teens overnight; that's awfully cold for a jacket. He's been out in it for nearly four hours, it can't be good. I want to check the ditches to make sure he didn't get hit by a car or something."

Now even more wide-eyed, Katee said, "I'm going with you."

"It's cold out. You just as well—"

"I'm going with you!" Katee shouted, throwing off the comforter. "I'll be ready in one minute."

"Okay, meet me downstairs."

Now was not the time to argue. Compromise was probably a better strategy; an extra pair of eyes might prove useful. Only… what if Katee were to see Ty crumpled in the ditch, half frozen, clinging to life, or even worse? The thought crossed both Deanne's and Thad's minds.

The respective calls were made. Mary Henry was instructed to stay in her house by the phone. Deanne was going to drive her car to the Henrys so she could stay with Mary. Thad and Katee would take a second vehicle, slowly retracing the route from the Henrys to the Thomases, carefully scouring the ditches for any sign of Ty.

Sheriff Dan Morris was relayed the message from Thad's call. The sheriff, along with Deputy Kyle Evans, would go to the Thomases in order to begin investigating Ty's disappearance.

Upon arriving at the Henrys' farm, Thad turned the driving over to Katee, instructing her to go ten miles per hour and to turn on the emergency flashers. He had their huge flashlight; with the window down, he had a good view of the ditch. Slowly, they traveled down the gravel road toward the paved county highway that led back toward the Thomases' house.

Katee sobbed slightly as they embarked on their mission. "I was going to knock on the Henrys' door to make sure Ty was there, but I didn't. God, I wish I would've."

"Don't beat yourself up now. Let's stay positive. We are going to find him and he'll be okay."

"We could have started looking for him four hours ago," she said. "If I hadn't been so concerned with Chaz and the damage to the door…"

"You don't need to worry about the damage to the door; I'll pay for that. In fact, I may even give Ty a medal for going to your rescue. What the heck, maybe I'll buy him a car."

Katee tried to keep from laughing. "Oh, Dad."

They turned onto the pavement. No sign of Ty. The security light at the Thomases' house could be seen from this intersection on a hazy day. This morning not only could it be seen, but the lights of two patrol vehicles could be seen as well.

The sheriff had awakened the boys: Chaz, Dave, and Luke; no one else was at the house. They had not seen Ty since earlier that night. Chaz gave his version. He had done nothing wrong and he wanted Ty to pay for the damaged door. Ty had sucker punched both he and Luke; he must have been drunk or on something—that was Chaz's story.

The sheriff knew Chaz pretty well, so he knew to take what he said with a "grain of salt" until he had all of the facts. The first priority was to locate Ty.

Deputy Evans was searching the area outside the house, when he made a discovery. "Sheriff, I've got something," he called on his radio.

"Be right there," was the reply. "I'll talk to you guys some more later. You just as well go back to bed for now." Sheriff Morris went to meet with his deputy.

The two officers visited about the discovery for not more than a minute, when Thad and Katee drove up, stopping on the highway. Thad got out, telling Katee to wait in the car while he talked to the sheriff.

"Dan…Kyle, we didn't see anything along the ditch on this side of the road." Thad offered what he knew, hoping the officers might have information they could share.

"Morning, Thad. Thanks for the call and coming out," Sheriff Morris said. "We may have something here. Kyle found some tracks leading into the timber."

Ty paused at the top of the steps after having walked out the front door of the Thomases' house. "If that don't beat all, I go in to try to save her, and she wants me to get the jerk some ice." Ty took a deep breath. He could feel the cold of the night air; somehow, it felt refreshing. From his pocket, he retrieved a stocking hat, put it on, and buttoned up his jacket. He didn't have any gloves, so he stuffed his hands into his jacket pockets. "I'm going home. If this is what she wants, she can have it."

Feeling a bit sorry for himself, he walked down the steps and out to the highway. After going a few yards, it occurred to him, *I could cut through the timber. It would save me a little distance, and it may even be warmer in the woods.* There would also be the added benefit of no traffic. In particular, a certain someone, realizing he was gone—as if she cared—might come looking for him, eventually.

Committing himself to taking the path through the timber, Ty selected an open entry point and left the highway for the woods. The snow was a bit deeper than what he had anticipated. He could feel the cold wet snow around his ankles. Oh, well. Maybe it wouldn't be so deep once he got into the timber.

Ty had been in this timber before, searching for mushrooms during spring break. That had been a couple years ago, before the accident that killed his father. They were in Iowa visiting GPa. Trace and Ty went on the search for morels as a lark. They never did find any, but had a good time looking. This fall, Ty hadn't had any reason to be in the timber. It was unfenced. A local developer owned the ground, but hadn't made any move toward actually developing it.

Ty discovered walking through the snow-covered timber in the dark and cold was a bit of a challenge. Not only did he have to navigate the underbrush, he also had to avoid getting lost. Following a straight line to his GPa's was a lot easier in theory than in practice.

He tried keeping his hands in his pockets for warmth. That seemed like a good idea, until he ran face first into a tree limb. Moments later he slipped, falling to a sitting position on the snow-covered ground. The snow wasn't as deep in the timber, just as Ty had anticipated. The trees caught a portion of it, preventing the snow from reaching the ground. Ty thought it felt warmer in the woods, perhaps deluding himself into thinking so. Regardless, it was still cold.

It is difficult to say exactly how far Ty had traveled into the timber, or for that matter, how erratic the path was that he took. He couldn't see very well, hardly at all, when suddenly it happened, without any warning; Ty's left foot found an opening of some description. He was in the process of stepping, putting all of his weight on the foot. He heard the snapping, crackling sound of wood as he fell, straight down at first. His foot becoming entangled in roots, he lunged forward. Now, he heard a second crack, a popping sound, the sound of bone breaking as his lower leg twisted. His foot had caught on the root of a tree as he fell into a ditch.

"Ugggh!" Ty exclaimed, startled by the suddenness of the fall and the shot of pain up his leg, not to mention the rough landing for his body in general. "Crap!" Ty clenched his fists, taking a couple deep breaths in an effort to gain his composure.

Some of the initial pain had subsided until Ty moved his leg, then he was quickly reminded that he was hurt. Assessing his situation, Ty discovered he had fallen into an odd-shaped ditch, almost like a sink hole enclosed on three sides. It may have been five feet deep, five or six feet wide, and ten feet long. He would later learn that there was a narrow opening on the fourth side. His foot caught on tree roots, awkwardly twisting his leg, apparently breaking a bone in the lower part of his leg. Gently he freed his leg from the roots. He carefully raised his pant leg, as best he could tell, there wasn't any bleeding.

Now, what to do? He was pretty sure that he could not continue through the woods tonight, given the trouble he had had up to this point. He could do better with the light of day, and that was giving no consideration to how difficult it might be to get out of the hole. It might help to splint the leg now rather than later. That may, he reasoned, prevent some swelling. Then he would need a crutch to get out of there.

"First things first," Ty said aloud. "It may help if I talk. Okay, so I need couple of sticks."

Feeling around, he found something. "Here we go. This should work." He broke the stick into two pieces. "Now, I need to be able to tie them together. Shoelace." He removed the shoe string from his left shoe. He slipped the ends of the sticks into his shoe on either side of his foot along the injured leg. "Okay. This may hurt a little." He let out a huge blast of air as he positioned the sticks and string. Clenching his teeth, Ty inhaled, then, exhaled as he tightened the string around the sticks, cinching the splint as tightly as he could make it about his lower left leg.

"Oh, baby, that really hurts." Shaking, he took deep breaths, allowing the pain to subside. "That's better."

"Not a lot better, but better. Now, what? Can't go to sleep, got to stay awake; keep talking. How am I going to keep from freezing?" Ty felt warmer in the hole than he did above the hole. Make no mistake, it was still cold, but it didn't feel as cold. "My leg is a little uphill. That should be good; maybe it won't swell. The leaves; I'll try to cover over with the leaves."

There were a lot of leaves that had collected in the hole; it seemed odd, or perhaps not so odd given the tree canopy, that there was not very much snow in the hole. Ty covered his legs and lower body with as many leaves as he could. He pulled his stocking cap down as far as it would stretch, covering his nose and lips. He retracted his arms from the sleeves of his jacket, folding them across his chest.

"Okay, so now what can I talk about? I can still wiggle my toes, might help a little. I suppose I could talk about Chaz; that might get me worked up. Or, I could talk about Katee. Ha, if Trace could only see me now, trying to think of something to talk about. Wouldn't that make her laugh?"

"Yep, it's going to be a long night. Maybe I should sing."

Katee could see the sheriff and his deputy getting into the trunks of their cars as her father returned to the car where she was waiting.

"Some good news, we think," Katee's dad said, getting in the passenger's side of the car.

Attentively, Katee listened, anxious for more information.

"They found some tracks. It looks like Ty went into the woods. He was probably trying to take a short cut home."

"But then he should have been home already."

"Unless he had trouble," Thad pointed out. "Sheriff Morris and Kyle are going to follow the tracks. We are going to go back to the Henrys and recheck the area in front of their house just in case."

The sheriff called for the ambulance to be on standby at the location where he and Deputy Evans were beginning their search. Katee and her dad drove back to the Henrys where they would look once more, this time focusing the search along the ditch to the west of the house, looking for signs where Ty may have come out of the woods.

They were at the Henrys' drive, stopping to allow Thad to get out of the car, when the sound of the ambulance siren split the dead of night. Katee instinctively clasped her hands together and whispered a prayer, "Please let us find him, and for him to be all right." A tear trickled from the corner of her eye. She dried it quickly with her gloved hand.

Her father reached over, patting her leg and reassuring, "Positive thoughts…positive thoughts." Thad got out of the car, walking a hundred yards or so, examining the snow in the ditch as he went. The snow in the ditch was not disturbed. It could only mean that Ty was still in the woods.

The sheriff had given Thad a radio to stay in touch in the event that he had discovered any tracks on the far side of the woods.

Thad reported that he found no tracks. He was instructed to wait, keeping a watchful eye, just in case Ty would happen to come out on that side. Convinced there was nothing more he could do, Thad rejoined Katee in the car. Laying the radio on the console between the seats, he noticed Katee's eyes were still full of tears, although she tried to put up a brave front.

"It'll be okay," he told her. "Now we just have to wait."

Katee nodded, afraid to speak for fear she would lose the tenuous grip she held on her emotions. She gripped the steering wheel, staring blurry-eyed through the side window. "Let him be okay. Let him be okay."

After putting on heavier winter gear, armed with flashlights and blankets, Sheriff Morris and Deputy Evans followed the tracks into the woods. They took turns calling into the darkness, "Ty!"

The ambulance arrived at the Thomases' residence. The EMT in charge called on the radio, "Sheriff, we're on site."

"Roger that," came the reply. "No sign of him yet. Stand by."

Katee and Thad could hear the sheriff's conversation on the radio that the sheriff had left with them. Thad reached down and turned up the volume to ensure they didn't miss anything. Silently, they listened, waiting, anticipating, praying for good news, better yet great news.

The sheriff and his deputy continued their search. They had the benefit of flashlights, allowing them to travel more easily than what Ty had, however, they were slowed following the tracks and periodically stopping to listen in hopes that Ty would respond to their calls.

After several minutes of trudging through the snowy woods, the sheriff said, "Wait a second," as he held out his arm. "I think I hear singing. Ty, are you there?"

"Yes, I'm over here. I'm in a hole." The reply was strained, but clear.

"Up there," the deputy said, excitedly leading the way. "We're coming."

Moments later the deputy and sheriff located Ty.

"Sorry to interrupt your song," the sheriff said.

"That's okay. I've already done that one five times. It's good to see you."

Several more minutes elapsed before the sheriff's voice broke the radio silence. Briefly startled by the sheriff's voice on the radio, Katee and her father held their breaths so as to not miss a word. "We've got him. He is awake and alert, but cold and his leg is hurt. We'll need the stretcher."

Katee high-fived her dad, then sniffled as she dried some more tears, tears of relief and joy.

"Better tell Mom and Mrs. Henry. Just drive up to the house."

Katee complied. Thad went in to share the news. He offered to give Mary and GPa a ride to the ambulance, which they accepted. Deanne would follow in her car.

The short drive to the Thomases was a quiet one. Katee parked behind the ambulance. An EMT who had been waiting by the ambulance approached the car. Katee rolled down the window for Mary.

The Henrys were acquainted with the EMT, Lucinda, from the hospital. "He'll be okay. We'll take good care of him."

"I know you will, Luce," said Mary, taking her hand as she reached into the car.

"You know he'll be okay. He's like his grandpa, too ornery to keep down," Lucinda said.

"You know that to be true," GPa said, as all in the car shared a chuckle.

"When they get him here, if you want to ride in with us, you're sure welcome."

"Yes, I'd like that."

Lucinda walked back toward the ambulance. Katee pressed the button to roll up Mary's window.

An awkward silence followed; it seemed to last forever. Forever that is, until Katee could stand it no longer. She felt as if she would explode.

"I am so sorry…this was all my fault." Her voice trembled with remorse, tears on her face.

Mary reached forward into the driver's seat, laying a gentle hand on Katee's shoulder. "Now don't you worry, Katee. I'm sure this wasn't all your fault. Ty will be all right."

"Yeah, don't worry child," GPa added. "Ty will be okay. He's a tough old dog."

Chapter Nine

"There they come." Thad was the first to announce that the team carrying Ty was in sight.

They all left the warmth of the car. Deanne met Katee and Thad just outside of their car. She put her arm around Katee, nodding to her that all would be well. Thad added his arm to the mix.

Mary and GPa went to the ambulance intently watching as the four men carried Ty out of the timber.

Katee tried to peek, just to get some sign from Ty to show that he knew she was there.

Ty was wrapped in the blankets, a cocoon providing warmth even though he was chilled to the bone. Quickly, he was loaded for transport to the hospital, Mary and GPa going along for the ride.

As the ambulance drove away, Thad approached Sheriff Morris, "How was he?"

"Could have been worse, I think he'll be okay though. They need to get him warmed up. He's pretty cold. Thought maybe he broke his leg too. I'm sure the docs will take good care of him."

Katee and Deanne moved to within earshot of the men.

"I told him we'd get some pretty nurses for him; that seemed to cheer him right up," the sheriff added for their benefit.

"I'll bet you did," Deanne smiled, squeezing Katee closer; her arm still around her shoulders.

Katee returned a toothless smile of her own. "I want to go to the hospital."

"You may not be able to see him for a while," her mother said.

"I don't care. I just want to be there so I can see him when I can."

"Okay, we'll go."

So the Robertses: Mom, Dad, and Katee would go to the hospital. It was nearly four a.m. Another half hour would pass before Mary appeared in the waiting room, filling them in on Ty's condition. There was no need to stay. Ty would not be able to have visitors until later in the day. It took some talking, but finally Katee was convinced to go home, get some more sleep, and freshen up before returning.

The buzz went around town quickly; Ty was in the hospital, nearly froze to death, having destroyed a door and punched out Chaz.

Shortly after noon, Katee and the Gang, including Chaz, gathered at the hospital to see Ty. Katee had ridden with Teej and Denny while Chaz had driven himself. Teej frowned at the presence of Chaz, but Katee greeted him warmly. Katee had texted him suggesting it would be good to bury the hatchet and show there were no hard feelings.

Teej wasn't so sure. She whispered to Denny, "Wish I still had that cane. You know what I mean?"

"Yes, I know what you mean. Control yourself."

Katee marched up to the nurses' station. "Hi, I'm Katee Roberts. We're here to see Ty Henry."

Politely, the nurse replied, "Great, I'll let him know you are here." Straightaway, she disappeared down a hallway. She was a stout-looking lady, friendly, in a no-nonsense way, easily someone's mother, perhaps a grandmother.

The nurse knocked on the door to Ty's room. "How are you doing?"

"I was just practicing my disco moves," Ty answered, tongue squarely in cheek.

"Good, you have your sense of humor. You have some company."

"Who would that be?"

"Katee Roberts and some others. One is Teej Hancock, I don't know the boys."

"Do I really have to see them? I'd rather not." Ty could see the nurse did not quite understand. "They'll ask a lot of questions. I don't feel like answering right now."

"Okay, Ace, I'll cover for you this time," she said with a wink. "Next time you are on your own."

Returning to the Gang, she informed them that Ty was still groggy from the medicine and wasn't in any shape to have visitors just yet. Perhaps they should come back tomorrow.

"Takes care of that I guess," Chaz said, then whispered to Denny, "Didn't really want to see him anyway."

Denny frowned at the comment. "He had a rough night. Maybe it is best that we wait and come back tomorrow."

"Yeah, maybe so," said Teej, seeing the disappointment on Katee's face. "We can come back tomorrow."

"I think I'm going to wait here a while. Maybe he will feel like some company later on. You guys go ahead and go. I'll call Mom when I'm ready to leave."

Not only was Katee disappointed, she was also stubborn. She took a seat, crossed her legs, and propped her head on her bent arm.

"You want me to stay with you?" Teej asked, not wanting to abandon her friend.

"Naw, you guys go ahead. I'll talk to you later."

They all said their good-byes. Teej gave Katee a hug. "I'll call you."

The time passed slowly. Katee found a couple of magazines, the kind you find in waiting areas. More than an hour passed, she had just finished perusing her third magazine when she saw Mrs. Henry in the lobby.

"Mrs. Henry," she called, eager to get her attention.

"Katee, have you been in to see Ty?"

"No, they said he was still groggy from medicine, so they wouldn't let me. Can you find out how he's doing?"

"I can do better than that. Come on, we'll give him a visit. I'm sure he wants to see you."

This is more like it, Katee thought.

Mary led the way. She knocked on the door to Ty's room, "You decent?"

"As long as you don't look at my backside; these hospital gowns don't cover everything real well."

Mary and Katee exchanged snickers.

"He must not be feeling too bad," Mary whispered. "Look who I found in the lobby."

"Hi," Katee said with a huge smile, hoping he would be glad to see her.

"Hi," Ty answered, a bit uncomfortable.

"How are you feeling?" Mary asked, placing her hand instinctively on his forehead, then taking his wrist to check his pulse. "How does the leg feel?"

"I'm good. The leg doesn't hurt as long as I don't move it," Ty answered.

"The pain killers must be working. The doctor said you did a good job with the splint, under the circumstances. I need to talk to them out front, so I'll leave you two to visit." Mary reached over kissing Ty on the forehead. "I'll be back in a few minutes. Don't let him try to get out of that bed."

"I won't," Katee said with a smile.

Katee squirmed as she turned back to Ty; her hands suddenly moist from a nervous impatience. "So…you're feeling better."

"Yeah, I'll be okay." Ty did not help matters with a smooth transition. "There's a chair, if you want to sit."

"Ah, yeah," Katee picked up the chair, moving it closer to the bed. "It's good that you're feeling okay. It must've been scary out there."

"A little."

Katee took a deep breath then exhaled with a blast of air. "We should probably talk about what happened if you are up to it."

"Sure."

Katee swallowed and began, "We need to do something about the damage to Chaz's door."

"Mom is going to talk to Mr. and Mrs. Thomas."

"Chaz was here today."

"I don't want to talk to Chaz," Ty said.

"Look, it would be good for you guys to talk and make a truce."

"I don't want to talk to Chaz. The guy is a jerk. If he doesn't know that's how I feel about him, then he's a stupid jerk."

"He was just joking," Katee said. "It wouldn't hurt you to say you were sorry for kicking in his door and punching him. If you just give him a chance, and get to know him—"

"No," Ty said, raising his voice. "I don't want to get to know him. I don't need to get to know him. And I sure am not saying I'm sorry; that's not happening!"

"He's one of my friends," Katee matched Ty's increased volume.

"Well, great! You can have him. You don't need to be hanging around me."

"Fine! I won't." Katee stood up abruptly, causing the chair she had been sitting in to topple backward.

"Fine," Ty said.

"Fine!" Consumed by the anger of the moment, Katee stormed out of the room. She made it, red-faced, to the lobby, through the front doors and into the parking lot before she realized she had no ride home. She was pulling out her cell phone when the first tears started to form and anger gave way to regret. *What just happened?*

Ty took his pillow in both hands, covering his face. He felt a sick empty hurt, and a couple of those annoying tears. "God, maybe I'm the jerk."

Teej and Denny stopped by the hospital the day after the blowup with Katee. Katee found an excuse not to go, and the two opted not to invite Chaz, mostly at Teej's insistence. They stayed for ten minutes or so making light conversation. Denny kidded that defenses couldn't stop Ty but a hole in the ground did. Teej offered to help with anything he might need.

"I suspect K will be at your beck and call. She probably won't let any of the rest of us do anything for you."

Ty shrugged, "I don't know. Thanks for offering to help. I'll try to not impose too much."

Teej had a small suspicion, but she was unsure of what. Something just didn't feel right, the way Ty acted, K not being able to come with them; it just didn't feel right. She shared her concern with Denny, but it was a mystery to him as well. So they left with a nagging feeling, a feeling that would only grow over the next few weeks.

The doctors decided that Ty would need a pin in his leg, a relatively minor surgical procedure, or so the doctor told his family while in the same breath warning that no surgery was minor. The surgery went well. Still, it kept Ty out of school for two weeks; assignments were delivered to him via email, his mom acting as courier when needed. When he finally went back to school, he used crutches to get around, a walking cast on his leg. Originally, the doctors wanted him in a wheelchair; he vehemently declined. A fellow student helped him with his books, navigating the halls between classes. Mostly, the helper would be Todd or one of the other football players. Occasionally, one of the girls helped, but never Katee, a fact that did not go unnoticed by classmates and teachers.

Ty fielded the barrage of questions as best he could. Most of the questions were from sympathetic fellow students and teachers who were concerned for Ty's well being. A few were from those with a morbid curiosity toward injury to the human body. Yet others would ask solely for the sake of asking; they just had to know. Although many would have liked to, no one asked what was going on between Katee and Ty. No one except for Teej. Teej would ask Katee for the story but never received a satisfying answer.

Secretly, Katee wished she could be a part of Ty's recovery, but she had botched their last encounter, or so she rationalized. She could be just as stubborn as he could be. If that was the way he wanted it, that's the way it would be. She didn't need to hang around him nor did Ty need to hang around her. She wouldn't care if he broke his other leg…no, she didn't wish that on him. She wanted to be a part of his world; why couldn't he see that? As for Chaz; he had always been a friend. Ty could at least try to be friends with Chaz, he didn't need to beat him to death.

It would be about that time the little voice of conscious would answer, "Oh, yeah, well you slapped Chaz for being a jerk. How is this any different?"

Katee would tense up, bent on not dignifying her inner thoughts with a response. Soon they would pass.

Teej knew something was wrong, but K wasn't talking.

"It doesn't matter," Katee would say.

"Yes it does," Teej would answer. "You're freaking me out. Something happened, so give it up. What's going on?"

"You can't do anything. Just drop it. Let's talk about something else."

This went on for three weeks.

It was Friday, the end of another week. The Gang, minus Chaz, was seated at a table in the commons area, awaiting the first bell of the day. The trio was very quiet, to the point of becoming bothersome, even for Denny.

Denny looked to Teej as if imploring, "Say something, anything!"

Teej tried to help. "K, have you picked a selection for speech contest yet?"

Not interested in the topic, Katee replied, "No, not yet."

Just then Chaz made his appearance, "Wassup ladies? Oh, you too, Denny. Didn't see you there." He snickered as he straddled a chair.

"Look, I've got to go. I'll see you guys…" Katee trailed off the sentence as Ty entered the commons on his way to his locker. She watched for a moment as he "three-wheeled it" on his crutches. As he moved out of view, she stood up and picked up her books.

As Katee walked away, Chaz said, "What's up with her? She's been like a zombie the past couple of weeks."

"I don't know. But I'm going to find out." Teej scooped up her books, leaving the boys behind. "Later."

Teej caught Katee at her locker, once again trying to pry some information out of her friend. "Are you going to tell me what's going on?"

"Nothing you can do anything about," Katee said, her voice with a certain unmistaken sadness.

The same old answer was still unsatisfactory to Teej, but she had another plan to find out what she wanted to know, so she did not press the issue.

It was time for Plan B.

At the end of math class Ty always packed up his materials five to ten minutes early in order to get to his next class before the rush of students filled the halls. Today would be no different.

"Is it okay if I go?" he asked Ms. Alnor.

She nodded yes.

Ty stood up and situated himself on his crutches.

As he did so, Teej followed suit. "I'll help you with your books this time."

Todd gave a surprised look, but Teej answered quickly, "It's time that I take a turn."

Katee also raised an eyebrow.

"Okay," Ty said with a slight frown. Yes, Teej had said earlier she would help Ty, but he didn't take her seriously. It didn't matter; he needed help with his books, so he would not complain.

He noticed Katee's reaction. Ty thought, *She must hate that, one of her friends bothering to help me*, a little uncharacteristic sarcastic pettiness on Ty's part.

As they made their way down the hallway, Ty said, "Thanks for helping me."

"You're welcome. Now you can give me some information. What's going on with you and Katee?" Teej asked, in a direct, no-nonsense manner.

"Maybe you should ask her."

"She's not talking and I'm sick of it. I'm carrying your books, so what's the deal?"

Ty sighed. "We had a fight. I might have said something I shouldn't have."

"So make up."

"She wants me to apologize to Chaz. That's not happening."

"She wants you to apologize?" Teej's face wrinkled with a look of consternation. "You don't owe him anything. He needs a swift kick at least once a week to keep him in line. Look, I have to go to the dentist in a few minutes; I'll talk to her tomorrow."

Ty rolled his eyes. "I'm not sure that will be helpful."

"Trust me, I'll make her listen."

Teej would spend the remainder of the day and evening mapping her strategy for broaching the matter with Katee. K was her best friend. She felt like she knew her better than anyone in the whole world. She knew that Katee could be stubborn and deathly loyal when it came to friends; that was good and bad at the same time. When it came to Chaz, Teej thought it was mostly bad, so she would need to approach the matter diplomatically.

Saturday morning arrived with a winter breeze that put an added nip in the air.

Keri was home for the weekend. She had arrived late Friday night, but arose early the next morning. At Deanne's request, she accompanied her mother to the grocery store. She hadn't been home since prior to the weekend when Ty was hurt, although she had been kept apprised of the goings on, at least from her mother's perspective. She had spoken with Katee, but Katee had side-stepped her feelings and the blow up with Ty.

This morning Katee was feeling sorry for herself. It had been the norm the past couple of weeks. The knock on the door should have brightened her spirits, it was Teej.

"Hi," Teej said cheerfully.

"Hi," Katee said. Her "Hi" sounded like a chore to say, although she managed a weak smile.

"Watcha doing?" Teej tried to ease into the conversation as Katee let her in.

"Nothing much. Dad had to work. Mom and Keri went to the store. What's going on with you? How was the dentist?"

"No cavities!" Teej made a celebratory fist pump.

"I need to talk to you about something." There was a pause. "I asked Ty what was going on with you two."

"I wondered why you wanted to carry his books."

"Yeah, well, I've been wondering why you haven't been. And you wouldn't tell me, so I asked him."

"And what did he say?" asked Katee, not wanting to sound too interested, even though she was.

"He said you wanted him to apologize to Chaz for what happened that night at Chaz's place."

"And he should." Katee's voice rose as if she were about to argue with Ty over this very topic.

"No he shouldn't. You know as well as I, Chaz can be the south end of a horse headed north. He needs to be responsible for his actions. I haven't heard any apology from him." The volume of Teej's voice increased, now matching, perhaps exceeding that of Katee's. Teej could feel her emotions rising; her face beginning to redden. She couldn't help herself; she had no intention of being bested in this argument.

"Chaz was just joking. You know how he does."

It wasn't so much what she said or that she was defending Chaz, but she turned her back to her best friend as she said it. Katee wasn't thinking. It was the match that ignited the fuel.

Teej felt like she was being ignored; dismissed as unimportant. Whether that was the case or not, did not matter. She erupted in an outburst of emotion and temper.

"You bet I know how Chaz does. I was there, Katee!" she shouted. "We didn't know what he was doing. Ty went to save you. He knocked those two guys out of the way. Denny and I were right behind him. I had a cane. I was ready to use it on anyone trying to hurt you." Her eyes were filling with tears; her voice sounded genuinely scared as she recalled the events of that evening.

Startled, stunned, Katee turned around. She was wide-eyed, her mouth open as if to speak but without the opportunity to do so.

"Don't you dare say it was just a joke! Don't you dare make excuses for him!"

Frustration overwhelmed Teej. "God!" she shouted, her hands to her eyes as she darted to the door.

"Teej…" Katee called meekly, but Teej was out the door, rushing to her car.

Katee stood for a moment in disbelief. "I can't believe that just happened!" That was her best friend; never had she spoken to Katee that way. Never had Katee seen her that emotional. First Ty, now Teej. Could things get any worse?

Katee sat on the couch, a sense of inescapable gloom surrounding her.

Keri and her mother came in the front door, carrying the bags of groceries they had purchased.

Katee did not move as the items were stored in the proper locations. She seemed impervious to her mother's and sister's presence. Had she been more cheerful, she would have offered to lend a hand, if for no other reason than to scope out the purchases. Not this time, though. This time, she remained deep in thought.

As the last items were put away, Mom whispered to Keri, "Talk to your sister."

Keri nodded, thinking, *If she's in her pouty mood again, how am I going to get her out of it? One thing's for sure, it needs to end. Ah, I've got an idea; here goes.* A light bulb had turned on. Keri was not convinced how well it might work, but a plan is a plan.

Sitting on the other end of the couch, an arms length from Katee, Keri picked up a magazine.

"How's it going, kiddo?" Keri asked as she opened the magazine, pretending to be interested in it.

With a heavy sigh, Katee replied, "Let's see. I lost my boyfriend and now my best friend. Pretty lousy, I guess." Katee was clearly in the dumps.

Lost her best friend? This must be new. One crisis at a time, Keri thought.

"So, you're not still going out with Ty?"

"Nope."

"So you and he are done, then?"

"Guess so."

"Mmm. Maybe I'll give him a call and see if he wants to go out with me."

This warranted a quick glance from Katee, a nearly imperceptible scowl that included an incredulous, "What?"

"We could go to the show or something. After that, who knows, maybe there will be some sparks."

"Get real. You're too old for him."

"Oh, please; I don't think so." Keri could tell that she had kindled a bit of life in her younger sibling. Now to milk it a bit further, "Maybe he needs the gentle touch of a more mature woman."

Katee went from lifeless self-pitying lump to raging ball of fury in a heartbeat.

"Mature woman? You've got to be kidding. You keep your grubby hands off him." Her voice raised to a shout; she swung a sofa pillow, striking Keri in her torso.

Keri retaliated, taking the pillow from her side of the couch and swatting her sister. "You don't want him. I'm going to take him. I'll show him what it's like to have a real girlfriend."

"Ah, here you two," Mom tried to intervene from the kitchen. Flustered, she felt the need to say something, although she wasn't sure what she should do.

"Like you'd know!"

The pillow fight was in full swing.

"I'll treat him a lot better than you have."

"I said keep your hands off," Katee shouted. Using the pillow like a club, she meant business. This particular blow went wide of its mark. Katee, who was by this time upright on the couch with a bent leg, lost her balance.

Keri took advantage of the miscue, and both girls toppled to the floor, Keri falling on top, straddling Katee, while clutching both of Katee's wrists, pinning her to the floor.

"Get off me, you cow," Katee bucked, struggling to free herself, but all to no avail.

"Don't think so. Not as long as you keep acting like a twit. So what gives; do you still want to be with Ty or not?"

Relaxing her futile efforts to escape her sister's grasp, Katee squeezed her eyes closed, forcing a tear from each of the corners. Sobbing she weakly answered, "Yes."

"Yes, what?"

"Yes, I want Ty to like me. Yes, I want to be with him."

"Okay then. Do you want my help?"

"What can you do?"

"Uh," Keri said. "You might be surprised. After all, I am tight with his sister."

She released Katee's wrists and swung herself from astride her sister.

"Besides, I know a few things." She extended a hand to Katee in order to help her up. "So let's start with Ty, give me the details."

Katee accepted Keri's hand; the girls now sat side-by-side on the couch. As Katee confided in her sister, the stress of the past few weeks gradually began to ease.

The storytelling took the better part of an hour.

"Okay, I think I've got the picture. Here is what we are going to do," Keri said in a take charge fashion. "First, you are going to call Teej and make up. Never… ever…let anything come between you and your best friend, unless it is something immoral. That's not what this is. It's okay to disagree, but that shouldn't get in the way of real friends, and you two are real friends. So you call her and make things right. I'm going to call Trace, then, we'll work on Ty. I already have an idea."

There was no argument from Katee, she eagerly retrieved her phone to call Teej.

"You called me a cow."

"I'm sorry. I didn't mean it. You called me a twit."

"Well, you were acting like a twit."

"And you felt like a cow."

The two girls laughed and made their phone calls.

Trace knocked on Ty's door, cautiously peeking into the room.

"Hi. Can I come in?" Not waiting for an answer, she went on in.

"Guess you can," Ty finally said. He was lying on his bed, propped up by two pillows. He had been reading a science book, part of an assignment.

"Doing a little light reading, I see."

"Could say that," Ty chuckled at his sister's observation. He nodded and smiled as he looked up from his book.

"So how have you been doing, Bubba? We haven't talked for a while. How's the leg?"

Ty reached down, tapping the cast, "Still got it."

"Does it hurt?"

"Nah, I can whack it pretty good and not feel a thing." Ty tapped the cast again, this time more sharply than before.

"Oh, I see. How about when I do this," Trace asked, pinching her brother's good leg.

"Ouch! Geez, Trace."

"Don't be such a smart aleck. I was being nice."

"Yeah, I know," he said rubbing the site of the pinch. "It hurts a little, but it's getting better."

"That's more like it. I got a call from Keri a while ago. What's going on with you and Katee?"

Now Ty squirmed. "There is nothing going on with us." His eyes turned away from his sister, wandering toward the window. He closed the book, now letting it become his focal point. He ran his hand over its cover as though cleaning it.

"So you're still going out, talking and everything."

"Not so much."

"Then what?"

"Oh, Trace." Ty knew that if he couldn't talk to his sister there was no one he could talk to. He also knew that he could not bluff his way past her, she would not allow it. He took a deep breath, then, blurted, "She likes frogs."

"What?" Trace did not want to sound indifferent, she didn't want her reaction to come out wrong, but she genuinely did not understand. "You mean, green little slimy long legged jumping frogs?"

"No," Ty shook his head, frustrated.

He took another exasperated deep breath, running his hands through his hair. "I mean two-legged croaking frogs." He pushed himself more upright on the pillows.

"Haven't you ever heard them? You get a bunch of them together and they all start croaking. They try to see which one can croak the loudest, and usually there is one. Once the loudest croaker has been established, the other little croakers don't seem to croak as loud—at least not in his presence. It's almost like they are taking notes or waiting for him to leave his throne so they can replace him as the king croaker. And you know what? Whenever he's not around, they croak as loud and as hard as they can, just looking for their opportunity."

Trace tried not to laugh, but she could not help herself. With a slight bit of laughter, she said, "I hadn't thought about frogs that way before."

Ty repositioned himself to a more prone position on the bed. "Well, you think about it, next time you see a bunch of people hanging out together, especially guys…I think Katee likes frogs, to be around them, to be the center of their attention."

Pushing himself up to a sitting position, he looked directly at Trace. "I'm not a frog, never will be one." Then he lay back.

Trace thought for a moment. She knew her brother as well as any sister could. There was a tone as he described the frog analogy that had a seriousness she realized should not be slighted. At this point in his life, a nerve had been touched for whatever reason. To disregard or down play it as without meaning would be hurtful to Ty. Trace could not try to laugh it off as a silly boy thing. There had to be a better way to help her friends, including her best friend, Ty.

Trace, who had been sitting at the end of the bed, stood up slowly.

"I think I see what you are saying… Have you ever considered that maybe Katee is just looking for her prince? I admit I've kissed a few frogs. Maybe Katee has too, trying to find her prince. What if you are her prince and she is your princess? Maybe you're not, I don't know. All I know is, when I had seen you two together, it looked right. When I've heard you talk about her or Katee talk about you, it seemed right. I'm not sure what that is." She placed her hand on his foot and shook it gently. "You just make sure, if you are going to write her off, that it is the right thing to do."

Trace left the room, leaving Ty speechless.

Ty would think about what Trace had said for the next couple of days. Whenever he happened to see Katee Trace's voice would seem to echo, "Make sure it's the right thing to do." Ty was now using only one crutch. He tried to use his leg as much as possible. Since it was the left leg that he injured, he was able to drive vehicles with automatic transmissions.

It must've been on Wednesday, or maybe it was Thursday; regardless, the economics/government class was in the library doing research. The last few days had been nice, temperatures in the high sixties—and here it was the last week of January. Indian summers in the middle of winter are not rare, but when they occur, they give a breath of fresh air that seems to say spring is on the way. Usually, a blizzard and record low temperatures follow—well, maybe not usually, but it feels that way. Anyway, this was a nice day and the class was in the library doing research.

Katee and Teej were sitting by themselves, sharing a table. They had made up on the weekend when Katee called. It was a tear-filled conversation with both girls apologizing and pledging to never let anything come between them. They both felt an overwhelming sense of relief as if a weight had been lifted from them. Other than Keri, no one knew of their crisis, nor did anyone else need to know. It would be their secret, a friends' secret of overcoming an ordeal, proving the strength of their bond.

The table was large enough to accommodate four students. Ty had just returned a book when he noticed Teej had left the table. He could see Katee remained, working, taking notes from a book. His mouth felt suddenly dry. *Make sure it's the right thing to do.* He closed his eyes for a moment. When he opened them again, he half expected to see that Chaz had moved over by her or perhaps that she had gone to the shelves or to the restroom; but no, Katee was still at the table by herself.

Ty whispered softly, "Okay Trace, here goes."

He took a magazine from a nearby shelf and went straightaway to where Katee was sitting. He glanced to see Teej preoccupied by a conversation with the librarian. Approaching the table, he asked so that only Katee could hear, "Mind if I sit here?"

Looking up from her work, pleasantly surprised, she awkwardly replied, "Uh, no." She pushed Teej's books to the side, making room for Ty. She unknowingly squirmed in her chair, sitting a little taller, adjusting her shirt to make it just so. Unconsciously, she swallowed, moistening her lips as she gave a quick glance toward Teej, just to see if she noticed the new arrival at their table.

Ty took a seat, propping his injured leg on another chair at the table. He made himself comfortable and pretended to skim the magazine for usable articles for his project.

The two exchanged a quick glance and a toothless smile, nodding as if to say, "Okay, here we are, sitting at the same table, now what?" Then, they returned to their work, mostly pretending to actually be doing something. It was hard for either of them to really concentrate.

By now, Teej had noticed Ty at the table. What was she supposed to do? She thought it best to not join them, so she loitered among the stacks of books, pretending to be looking for something. Mercifully, the bell rang, signaling the end of the period.

Instinctively, Katee began to collect her belongings. "Do you need help with your books?" she asked hurriedly.

"Nah…I can get them. I've got a free hand now," Ty said lightheartedly, waving his right hand. Fidgeting, unsure of what the response might be and not wanting to be disappointed, he continued, "Look, I have to pick up Grandpa's truck at Jackson's after school tonight. I was wondering, since it's nice, would you walk with me? I kinda wanted to talk to you." Jackson's was an auto repair shop a few blocks from the school. Hastily, he added, "I'll buy you an ice cream."

Katee smiled. "Can't say no to ice cream." There was something about just talking to Ty again that gave her a warm feeling. It was as though their fight had never happened. Maybe now, everything would be okay. Maybe, just maybe, Keri's connection with Trace had come through. Even so, Keri had warned her, "I can only do so much; the rest will be up to you. And if it doesn't work out, just let it go and move on. There are other guys in the world."

True, sis, there are lots of guys in the world, but there is only one Ty, Katee thought. *"I can't explain it. I've had crushes before, boyfriends who I thought were special. Ty is different; he's got a heart. He's…"*

"Great! Meet you at your locker right after school?"

"Sure."

Ty went on his way. Teej caught Katee at the table. Teej didn't say a word, but she had that inquisitive look.

"He wants me to walk up town with him after school, get an ice cream, and talk." Katee shrugged. "Guess we'll see."

The remainder of the day would seem to drag for both Katee and Ty, each trying to anticipate what they would say and how to respond to what the other might say.

Finally, the dismissal bell rang. The mad rush in the halls followed. Katee went directly to her locker. She did not want to be late, although it crossed her mind that it might be good if Ty had to wait on her just a bit. Ty had never been late for any of their meetings before, so she wouldn't make him wait this time. Once she was there, the urgency slowed considerably. She meticulously stored her books, keeping a choice few to take home for the evening. Other students around her banged their lockers, tossing books in with a careless fervor that made one wonder what the rush was.

Within minutes, as quickly as the mass of humanity had filled the hall, the numbers dwindled, chaos giving way to a more sane and tolerable manner of conduct.

Katee stood with her back against her locker, her book bag slung over one shoulder. She could see Ty coming down the hall. He stopped at his locker briefly, then, continued toward Katee.

"I'm coming," Ty called, still yards away.

"No hurry," Katee said with a smile.

Ty joined her moments later.

"I need to put my bag in my car," Katee said.

"Good idea."

Just then Teej and Denny happened to walk by them. Katee held up crossed fingers, concealed so that only Teej could see.

Teej nodded slightly in acknowledgment. "I'll call you."

As they moved out of earshot, Denny asked, "What's going on there?"

"I'll find out when I talk to K later tonight," Teej answered. "Just hope it's good news."

The walk downtown was a pleasant one. The warmth of the day made a light jacket feel comfortable even though there were signs of winter still everywhere, dried brown splotches of grass surrounded by banks of snow, albeit melting snow, on this day. Ty and Katee's conversation on the way to the car shop was light, perhaps a little awkward at times. It suited Katee just fine. She wasn't anxious to relive their argument. If they could just pretend it never happened and move back to the way it was before that winter night, she would be good with that. Somehow, she feared that was not quite what Ty had in mind when he said he wanted to talk to her. The truth of the matter was, she knew they needed to talk, air their differences and reach a mutual understanding; then and only then could they restore what had seemed to be a blossoming relationship.

They picked up Ty's grandfather's pickup and took the short drive to the ice cream parlor. They ordered and settled into a booth, sampling their respective selections.

Ty took a deep breath then said, "I …ah…I've been thinking about what happened at the hospital…a lot."

"Me too," Katee said, stirring her ice cream gently, as if to create some artistic masterpiece.

"Look, Chaz's dad told Mom that he didn't want anything for the door. He said Chaz wasn't supposed to have anyone over, so, I guess he got in trouble."

"I didn't hear about that."

"I know he's your friend and everything. I just don't like the guy."

"I know…I know."

"Well. When I thought he was hurting you…."

"I get that now, too. Teej made me see. I was just worried because he was talking about calling the police and the door was smashed and he was bleeding and…." Katee got a little excited. She noticed Ty was playing in his ice cream, staring at it, avoiding eye contact with her.

"And he's your friend. I'm not apologizing. I don't want to be his friend."

There was a long pause in the conversation, then, Ty added, "So where does that leave us?"

Now it was Katee who took the deep breath. "Well, let's see." She took a paper and pencil from her hip pocket. She had stored them there in anticipation of this moment. Unfolding the paper, she wrote their names at the top of two columns.

"Okay, here's how this will work," she said. "We take turns. If I have a reason we should hang out, I get one point. If you have a reason we should hang out, you get a point. Likewise, we get points for any negative, a reason why we shouldn't hang out. When we get done, if the point totals are close, the one who is behind can do something to catch up and we keep seeing each other."

"If they are not close," she said weakly, "We forget it and see someone else."

She hesitated, waiting for a response from Ty.

"O…kay," he said deliberately.

"Okay, so here we go," Katee said. "I like you. So I get one point." She made a mark beneath her name, then looked to Ty. "Now it's your turn."

"I like you too."

"Good. You get one point." Katee made a mark in Ty's column. "That makes us even," she said with a hint of contentment. *This would be a good time to stop*, Katee thought.

"I didn't get to go to homecoming. That should be two points. Right?"

Katee wrinkled her face, clenching her lips together. "Point and a half."

"You didn't say anything about fractions of a point, so it has to be two, since it is certainly more than one. And do you put them as minuses or pluses?"

"Pluses. And okay, you'll get two points," Katee said, marking the points in Ty's column. "I made pies, so that's two points for me."

"But you only had to make one."

"But I had to learn how to make the pie, so I deserve two points for the extra effort involved."

"Okay, okay. You get two points." Ty laughed, taking a bite of ice cream.

Katee laughed in return, "Don't you try to cheat me out of a point."

"Uh…I'm just learning this game. How can I cheat?"

And so it went. What was to be an exercise to see whether the two should continue to have a relationship with one another became a game, a game that brought the two back together. There were other issues; I don't like Chaz. You do like Teej and Denny. You ran out and left me at Chaz's without saying you were leaving. I went with you to Chaz's in the first place. And so on.

Finally, when all had been vented, Katee tallied the scores. "You have nineteen. I have eighteen. That's nothing. I can make a pie." Her face had certain glow of satisfaction with the results.

Ty reached across the table, taking her hand, "How about we make a pie together? And you can choose what kind."

"Better yet. I say chocolate. Oooo, or French Silk." A huge smile filled Katee's face.

At that moment, Teej and Denny entered the parlor. Teej couldn't resist checking in on the progress of her bff. She knew they were going for ice cream, so she hoped maybe K would flash a sign as to how things were going.

To Teej's delight, Katee gave her the thumbs up sign. She didn't even try to conceal it. Not that it mattered; Teej could tell by the look on Katee's face that all was going well. Teej whispered to Denny, "They're back."

Chapter Ten

All was right with the world. Ty and Katee had mended the fence, resuming the way things were prior to the winter incident. Ty's leg was healing, although realistically he knew a run at a state championship would not be likely. In fact, he may not be able to run track at all this spring.

Katee tried to help him remain optimistic. She still felt as though she had played a part in the mishap. To her way of thinking, it was her fault that Ty missed out on the homecoming event and now the pursuit of the track championship, both of which meant a lot to him.

Ty tried to alleviate her concerns. "Let's move on and not worry about things we can't do anything about," he had told her.

"You might heal quicker than they think," Katee said. "Don't give up. What's the saying? 'It's not over 'til it's over.' You just have to believe and do your best."

"Okay. That's good advice." Ty could hear a little of his parents and sister coming from Katee.

"You're darn right," she said with a wink. "And I'll help."

Together, the two would exercise, Ty doing what he could and Katee joining in. The exercising had to be scheduled around all of the other conflicts, but somehow they managed. It wasn't long before Ty no longer needed a crutch; it was a bit longer before he was able to have the cast removed.

Katee had convinced Ty to try out for the spring play. He received a small part. He was glad to have gotten involved, if for no other reason than it gave him an excuse to be around Katee all the more. Even so, he did not see himself as an actor. Katee, on the other hand, was a natural, but that is another story.

The play was a rousing success. Performances were held on the two evenings prior to spring break, which was the last week in March. It was during that week away from school Ty stopped by to see Katee. They took a walk, talked a ton, and were now listening to music. Ty could tell something was on Katee's mind, exactly what, that was the mystery.

Finally, he decided it was time. "So, are you going to tell me? 'Cause I don't think I can guess."

"Tell you what?"

"Whatever it is you are thinking about."

Katee gave him the look, her lips tightly held together, holding back a full-fledged smile, her eyes with an unmistaken wide-open innocence.

"Follow me," she said after a thoughtful pause. She led the way to the family computer. She turned it on, sat down, and instructed, "Have a seat." There was a hint of mischievous red in her face, obvious even to Ty.

Ty took a chair in front of the machine.

"Now go to the school's website."

Ty did as instructed. Clicking the mouse, he glanced at Katee.

"Oh brother." He laughed. "I'd better not screw this up, had I?"

"Nope," she burst out in response, now smiling. "I'm going to help you. It'll be okay. Now go to the activities calendar; it's there at the top."

Ty wiped his hand across his face. "Okay, got to get serious. I can figure this out, whatever it is."

"I'm sure you can. You are looking for something in April."

"Something in April…I see a track meet."

"Nope, that's not it."

"There's a golf meet."

"Still not it."

"Hmmm…oh, there's an early dismissal."

"No," Katee said curtly, wrinkling her brow. "Stop messing around."

"Well, the only other thing I see is prom," said Ty as he looked at Katee out of the corner of his eye to watch her reaction.

She took a long deep breath. "Yes, you knew all along!" Her face turned red. She cocked her head to one side, her eyes open wide.

Ty couldn't help but laugh.

"What's so funny?" said Katee, folding her arms.

"Nothing." Ty composed himself. "Say, would you go to prom with me?"

Now it was Katee peeking out of the corner of her eye to see Ty's reaction, a huge smile engulfing her face. "Yes…It took you long enough," she said, poking him playfully on the shoulder.

"I'm kinda slow," Ty said. "Sometimes I need a nudge."

"Uh huh. I know what you mean." Then she laughed.

Later that week Ty invited Katee to join his family for pizza, followed by an evening of Monopoly. Katee had accepted. She felt as though she was getting to know all of Ty's family and feeling very comfortable around them.

They had eaten most of the pizza and the Monopoly game was in full swing with Mary, Trace, Katee, and Ty all joining in. GPa opted out, insisting that it would be best to have an impartial observer in case there were any disagreements; that way he could mediate. The game was going well. Everyone was having a good time.

"I've been thinking," Ty said during a lull in the action.

"Oh, no! Not that," Trace said.

Ty flashed his sister a brotherly frown while the others giggled. "I have good thoughts, on occasion," he said, undaunted by the sisterly ribbing. "In fact, this is a fantabulous idea. I think we should do something cool for prom."

"Oooooo…this sounds intriguing." Katee's interest had been aroused. "Tell us more."

"Well, I saw Todd downtown yesterday. He said there is a drive-up where everyone kind of makes an entrance. He said that everyone tries to have a novel way of driving up, like someone brought a semi-tractor one time. Well…I'm thinking the 'B.'"

"What?" Trace and Mary said in unison.

Not quite sure how to react, Katee had that uneasy look about her. She didn't want to dash Ty's enthusiasm, but the reaction of his sister and mother to this "B" idea was a little disconcerting.

"What's a 'B'?"

She didn't really direct the question at anyone in particular, but looked toward Trace as well as Ty. She hoped that the sister would have her best interest at heart.

"It's a Farmall. It's a tractor. It has a side seat that you can sit on, and I'll drive. It'll be great!"

Trace shook her head. "Why don't you just take Mom's car or…" Trace looked at Katee.

"We could ask about borrowing my cousin's car. He just got a new Camaro."

"The 'B' will be so much cooler."

"Oh, I don't know, Ty," said Mary. "Katee might not want to ride on that side seat in a formal. It might not be safe."

GPa felt the need to chime in on Ty's behalf. "You know what you could do? Clean up the old seeder cart and pull it behind the 'B'. That would take care of the safety issue."

"That old thing has iron wheels," Mary said.

"You won't be going very far. It wouldn't be bad," said GPa.

"Yeah, I'll paint everything. It'll be great."

Katee did not know what to say. She did not want to burst his bubble, but the expressions on Mary's and Trace's faces did not give her a great deal of confidence. After all, this was her senior prom too.

"You only have, like, three weeks," Trace said in one last attempt to dissuade him from the idea.

"Yeah, I know. I can do it. It'll be great. You'll love it." Ty winked at Katee.

Katee returned a weak smile.

Trace leaned toward Katee. In a half whisper that was intentionally loud enough for all to hear, she said, "He'll never get that 'B' running. Ask about the Camaro."

"Have a little faith. Whose turn is it?"

The game continued without further reference to prom, the "B," or the seeder cart. Katee bit her lip. She would have liked to have discussed this notion of the drive-up a bit more thoroughly. In fact, she would like to see this seeder cart before agreeing to ride in it. Then again, Ty was excited. Oh well. How bad could it be?

The next week was back to school; the final countdown was on for the seniors. There were those who were afflicted by senioritis, an ailment that affects a senior's ability to focus on academic work. Both Katee and Teej were showing some symptoms, but their cases appeared to be mild. Ty and Denny seemed to be unaffected, while Chaz proudly boasted of having contracted the disease as a freshman. Regardless, spring was definitely in the air.

Teej and Katee were at a table in the commons before school along with Denny, bemoaning a paper that was now due on Friday. Katee had the first page done, Teej the first paragraph.

"So you want to come over tonight and we'll work on it?" Teej asked.

"Ha. We wouldn't get anything done. Best we work on it ourselves. You can call if you have questions." Katee was being honest. "Say, speaking of questions, I just thought of one. Do either of you know what a seeder cart is?"

"It's like a wagon, used to sow seed and fertilizer," Denny answered.

"With iron wheels, right?"

"That would be a really old one. Why are you asking?"

"Ty wants me to ride in one to prom."

"Oh…my…gosh." Teej's jaw dropped open.

"What's he going to pull it with?" Denny asked. He seemed to think it was a better idea than what the girls did.

"He has a tractor, a 'B'; whatever that is."

"That could be cool."

"Oh, yeah… Do you and Teej want to ride with us? You can be on the tractor with Ty and Teej can sit in the seeder cart with me."

"Not so fast," Teej said quickly. "You know I love you, K… but…there are limits."

"Oooh, I was afraid you'd say that." Katee rubbed her forehead with both hands. "What am I going to do?"

"Do about what?" Chaz asked as he approached the group.

"Ty's going to take her to prom with a 'B' and a seeder cart. I think it's a neat idea," Denny said, despite receiving a sour look from Teej.

"You're kidding! Just what I'd expect from a redneck."

The comment received disgusted looks from both Katee and Teej.

Oblivious to their reactions, Chaz continued, "That's easy to get out of; just pull the distributor cap. You could take a plug wire, but he might have a spare one of those. I doubt he has a spare distributor cap lying around. You want me to slip over the night before and take care of it?"

"No," Katee said flatly. "I don't."

Chaz winked at Denny. He took such pleasure in pestering the girls.

Denny chuckled with a shake of his head. *Another great idea from Chaz.*

Later that day, Teej and Katee were alone, walking to Teej's car, when Katee asked, "Do you know what a distributor cap is?"

"Nope, never heard of it before today. Are you thinking what I think you might be thinking?"

"Oh, no. It's more like worried. What if Chaz goes ahead and does something? You know it would be just like him."

"Ya think?"

"Yes…I do think."

"Maybe you should warn Ty."

"Then he'll know we were talking about it."

"So…I don't think that will be a big surprise. It's prom, after all. Why wouldn't we be talking about it? That's no big deal. But if Chaz does something stupid and Ty finds out you knew about it beforehand, that wouldn't be good."

"You're right. You're right. You…are so right. I'll go over to Ty's tonight."

There was a sense of relief in discussing with a friend and deciding on a course of action.

"That's what I'll do. Maybe I can sneak a peek at the seeder cart just to see how it's coming along."

Teej couldn't help but laugh. "Good idea."

It was about 5:30 that evening when Katee pulled into Ty's drive. She could see him by the barn. Getting out of her car, she waved and called to him, "Hello."

"Hi. I didn't know you were coming by this evening," Ty said as Katee walked toward the barn.

"I thought I'd surprise you. How's the seeder cart and tractor coming?"

"Ah. So that's what you have on your mind."

"Well…you've had a week; it'll be here before you know it. I just wanted to see how it was going, first hand."

"It's coming along. You don't get to see it, though. I want it to be a surprise."

"No…I don't like surprises."

"I see. You just like to spring them. Well…you're going to have to wait."

"But I could help. I can paint while you work on the tractor."

Ty seemed to ignore the comment. "Hey…there is something you could do: make a sign for the back. It could say something like 'Prom: Here We Come.' What do you think?"

"Okay." Katee sighed. "I can do that. How big and what colors?"

"About three feet by two feet would probably work. If you use white poster board, you can use whatever colors you want for the lettering and it will look good."

"What color is the seeder cart? Surely, you can tell me that."

"Black, but that is all you get to know."

"Hmmmm, so that's all I get." Katee said disappointingly. Then she smiled before saying—trying to make it sound like an afterthought, "There is something I should tell you. We were talking about prom, and I mentioned the 'B' and seeder cart. Well, Chaz was there, and you know how Chaz is."

Katee fidgeted; this was harder to get out than what she had imagined it would be.

"Anyway, he said he might slip over and swipe the distributor cap from the 'B.' I don't even know what a distributor cap is, but I told him not to."

Katee looked at Ty to gauge his reaction.

Ty folded his arms, trying not to laugh. The look on Katee's face was priceless. "Don't worry about it. The 'B' is locked up. But if he should get to it, I have a new cap that I won't put on 'til I need to."

"I just wanted you to know in case he tries something. I didn't have anything to do with it."

"That's good to know. I'm glad you told me. If I were Chaz, I wouldn't try it, though. Grandpa keeps a shotgun, loaded with rock salt, by his bed. I doubt that it would do any permanent damage to a person, but Grandpa has always said it really stings for several days."

"I'll mention it to him."

They both laughed.

The next couple of weeks seemed to fly by. Ty and Katee didn't spend a lot of time together; the preparations for prom got in the way, plus every teacher seemed to be piling on the homework, trying to cover as much as possible before the seniors' last day.

Before they knew it, the "big day" had arrived. Katee asked Ty on Friday how work was going on the "B" and seeder cart. She made a point of reassuring him that her cousin's Camaro would be in the drive, just in case there were any problems, so they had a backup plan.

"That's good to know. Always a good idea to have a backup plan," Ty answered.

"Yep, that's the way I see it, always good to have a backup plan. So, is the 'B' running?"

"Like a top. Purrs like a kitten."

Katee heaved a deep sigh. "See you tomorrow, about four o'clock. Mom wants to take some pictures before we go. If your mom or Trace wants to come over and take pictures, they're welcome."

"I'll ask and see what they say. I know they plan on getting some pictures at the drive-up."

Katee nodded understandingly. "We can always make copies, so we should be good."

"Yeah…a backup plan for the pictures," Ty grinned.

"Are you making fun of me?"

"No…not at all."

On Prom Saturday, Ty was prompt as usual. He wore a nice suit, opting to not spend a small fortune on a tuxedo. Katee wore a red formal, very stylish and in Ty's eyes radiantly beautiful.

Katee's parents and Keri were on hand for the picture-taking ritual leading to the send off of the well-dressed couple.

Katee greeted Ty at the door. "Hi, right on time."

"Hi…you look fantastic," Ty managed to say while offering Katee the corsage he had brought.

"She should for what that dress cost," Keri chimed in.

"That is the dress you wore a couple years ago," Keri's mother said.

"Oh…yeah, I remember. That's how I know what it costs…I looked pretty good in it too."

"You are so modest. That's what I like about you, sis." Katee said. "I did have to take it in a little." Quickly she added, "Just kidding. Help me with this." Katee handed the corsage to her sister. "Please."

"Mmmph," Keri grunted indignantly as she expertly affixed the flower to the dress. "Now, you two stand over there so I can get some pictures. Mom and Dad, get ready. I want you in a picture too."

"Yes, ma'am," Thad replied, saluting as he did so.

"You're not funny. Comb your hair," Keri said.

The photo-taking lasted about fifteen minutes. It would have taken ten, but the good-natured silliness slowed the process down. Finally, Katee turned to Ty, the impatience clearly starting to show, "Guess it's time to get going. Did you notice the Camaro in the drive? It matches my dress." She tried to keep from laughing, but Ty could recognize the teasing.

"Uh…you're not having second thoughts about the seeder cart are you?"

"Oh, no," Katee answered, fearing she may have said the wrong thing. "I'm just kidding. I'm good with the seeder cart. We can go on the backs of donkeys if you want."

"Donkeys…really! That's an idea. The Millers have some donkeys," he said excitedly.

"No, no, no. Just kidding. The seeder cart will be fine."

Ty chuckled. Somehow, he felt he had gotten the better of the exchange.

"You two had best get going, before you get into a fight and don't get going at all," Deanne said. "We'll be at the drive-up." She gave Katee a kiss on the cheek. "Be careful not to snag your dress."

"I will," Katee said.

Ty held the door for Katee, allowing her to slide into the passenger side of his mother's car. She fastened her seat belt, the excitement of the moment giving her that warm feeling of anticipation that a person gets before a big event.

Ty climbed in behind the wheel on the driver's side, fastening his seat belt. "You sure you're okay with the seeder cart?" he asked with a smile. The look on his face gave away the eagerness he felt for an affirmative response.

Katee was not going to crush his moment. "Yes…I'm sure. It's going to be great."

"All right…You have to put these on."

"Sunglasses…You painted the lenses!"

"Yep…I don't want you to see what I did until you get out of the car." Ty backed the car into the street and they were on their way.

"Oh, my gosh. These are like a blindfold," Katee said as she slipped on the sunglasses. "This is so weird. I can't see a thing."

"That's the idea. We'll be there in just a few minutes. Trace suggested that I just have you wear a paper bag. I thought this way it wouldn't mess your hair."

"Ah, I agree. Good thinking on your part. The paper bag idea sounds like a Keri suggestion. Did those two talk?"

"Possibly. I can't say for sure though." Ty stole a glance at Katee. "You really do look fantastic. But then, you'd look good in a gunny sack."

"Ha…wish I had that paper bag. You wouldn't be able to see me turn so red."

"Ah, that's okay. I'm mostly watching the road. We are almost there. Remember…you can't take the glasses off until I say to. I'll help you out of the car and tell you when."

"Okay, I got it. Maybe I'll keep them on all evening. They're kind of stylish."

"Then you wouldn't be able to see anything. Here we are." Ty slowed and turned off the main street. "Remember, no peeking."

"No peeking. I promise."

Ty got out of the car and hurried around to Katee's side. She had unfastened the seat belt without assistance. Ty helped her out of the car. She clung to his right arm as he led her around the front of the car and what seemed like twenty yards to the designated spot where Ty wanted her to be.

"Okay," Ty freed his arm from Katee's grip and placed his hand gently on her back. "Now…you can take off the glasses."

With both hands, she grasped the temples of the sunglasses, slowly removing them in order to allow her eyes to adjust to the change in light.

"Oh my gosh!" Her jaw dropped, her eyes widened. "Oh my gosh…Oh my gosh!" She was oblivious to Trace snapping pictures and Mary videotaping the moment. Speechless, she reclaimed Ty's arm, squeezing it tightly with both hands. At last she was able to ask, "How?" The look on her face seemed to complete the sentence.

"That's not the seeder cart. Hope you're not disappointed," Ty smiled, basking in the satisfaction of Katee's unrehearsed reaction. The glow on her face was his reward; this was great. Regardless, he felt like he had "done good."

No…it was not the "B" and the seeder cart. It was Chastity, the white mare. GPa, dapperly dressed in tails and a top hat, stood by her head, tenderly stroking her nose. Her mane was neatly cut, her hair snowflake white. Her bridle and harness were all black, trimmed with chrome that glistened in the afternoon sun. She was hitched to a covered carriage. The carriage was black with ornate designs that gave it a regal appearance.

"No…not at all. But where did you get the carriage?"

"It's Grandpa's. He keeps it in the barn, covered up. There was a time when newlyweds would use it. Remember, I told you that Chastity was a harness horse. It's been a few years, but she remembers how it's done. We've tried her out. She's good to go."

"It's beautiful. This is so neat!" She squeezed his arm more tightly. "And you knew all along." The expression on her face was priceless.

"I'm glad you think so. I put your sign on the back. It looks good."

They stepped to the rear of the carriage. There was a frame built onto the carriage to hold the sign. Ty explained that GPa had made it for when newly wedded couples used the carriage. They liked to put a sign saying "Just Married" on the back of the carriage. This time it held the sign that Katee made, "Prom: Here We Come."

"Oh my gosh, it does look good. I think the carriage makes it." Katee was still in awe.

GPa, now standing by the door of the carriage, winked at Ty, who acknowledged with a slight nod of his head. Removing his hat while making a huge bow and sweeping gesture with his left arm, GPa announced, "Your carriage awaits, My Lady."

Katee laughed, allowing Ty to escort her to the side of the carriage. All the while, Trace and Mary were filming.

As Katee stepped onto the carriage step, Trace instructed, "Pause and smile for the camera." Smiling was not a problem. Katee could not help herself.

Ty helped Katee into the carriage, followed her in, and took his place by her side. Trace and Mary bolted to the car in order to hurry to the school for the drive-up.

GPa removed the anchor that held Chastity and took his place in the driver's seat.

"Here we go," he called to his passengers. Next he made a clicking sound. Chastity performed on cue, starting at a walk, then quickening to a trot.

"We're on our way," Ty said, taking Katee's left hand with his right.

"Yep," Katee said, still bursting with the excitement of the moment. She surveyed the interior of the carriage. "This is so cool! I can't believe you did this…and you kept it a secret, making me think that we were taking a seeder cart. Your whole family was in on it!" Katee's eyes widened at the realization.

"Not the entire time. GPa was the first to know. Mom and Trace, I had to swear to secrecy. I was afraid Trace might let it slip to Keri, but she had to know to help take pictures."

Katee chuckled at the thought, took another look around the carriage, and then made up her mind. With one motion, she turned to Ty, pulling him gently to her and kissed him full on the mouth for the very first time.

This time, it was Ty who was surprised.

Katee released his neck, slightly embarrassed. She turned back toward the front of the carriage and looked out the window. "Had to do that. Hope you didn't mind."

"Ah…no, that was fine. Kind of liked it actually."

They both laughed.

Their arrival by carriage got the attention of most and the envy of many. Katee's parents were impressed; they really liked this Ty Henry. Teej was jealous, good-naturedly so. Keri gave Trace a hard time for not filling her in. The pictures and video were marvelous. They would be displayed prominently at graduation celebrations a few weeks later.

For many couples, prom is more the end than the beginning. Not so, for Ty and Katee, for them it is only part of the story. That shouldn't be surprising, not when you've got a love'n heart.

The following is for all of my former students who would expect me to include some verse.

Got a Love'n Heart written by L. Martin

Got a Love'n Heart,
    Got a Love'n Soul.
Every song I sing,
    Everywhere I go.

Oh, what a lovely feeling,
    Girl, what you do to me.
Oh what a lovely feeling,
    Comes so naturally.

Place your hand in my hand,
    Press your lips to mine.
Know that I will love you,
    Forever and all time.

I will never leave you,
    The taste of love's too strong.
'Long as you will have me.
    Here's where I belong.

Got a Love'n Heart